Little Bird

CRIMINALLY YOURS

TAYLOR JADE

To finding someone who loves you like Easton loves his little bird.

Prologue

EASTON

Four Years Ago

The streets were eerily quiet tonight.

The lamplights flickered above, barely lighting a path for us. Mosquitos buzzed in our ears, and humidity weighed us down a little more with every step. Beads of sweat lined my forehead and dripped down my back, clinging to the thin fabric of my t-shirt.

Summers in Florida were brutal during the day, but somehow, they were even worse at night when a warm breeze would brush my sticky skin, bringing the promise of another unbearably hot day ahead.

"Boss said it's our last run." Gray's hoarse voice filled the silence with a puff of smoke from the cigarette between his fingers.

"He says that every time," I reminded him, studying his ashen face before checking our surroundings. I buried my hands deeper into my pockets, my fingers curled around a blade, just in case someone tried to attack us.

Anything was possible in this part of town.

"I told him we were done. I've got a baby on the way. I can't keep doing this shit anymore." He coughed, lungs wheezing for air, but instead of breathing in clean oxygen, he stuffed the cigarette back between his lips, inhaling the poison.

I wanted to tell him that he should quit smoking, but we'd had the same argument since we were kids, and now at twenty-two, it wasn't my job to take care of him anymore.

I needed to get out of this stupid arrangement more than he did. He might have a baby on the way, but I had my future on the line. With a business degree under my belt, I spent the last four years grafting my ass off at a local construction company with hopes of working my way up the goddamn ladder.

My foreman promised me a raise when I graduated. With my diploma out in the mail, I was guaranteed a better life.

"I'm not fighting you. I've wanted out for a long time. I'm tired of looking over my shoulder every goddamn day." Speaking of, I checked behind us to make sure we weren't being followed, and he did the same. It had become a habit over the years. We both had scars from runs gone wrong.

"I can't be caught up in this shit. I still haven't told Anna." He mentioned his pregnant girlfriend, the one that was far too good for the likes of him, but I didn't say anything. He never listened to me anyway.

"Where does she think we are?" Thunder loomed above, lightning crackling in the dark sky.

"Told her we were going for drinks." He threw the butt of his cigarette to the ground and stuffed his hands in his loaded pockets.

He always carried the poison, and I always carried the cash. We were a good team. Coming from the same foster home, we weren't new to the life of dealing, but it didn't mean we liked it either. We did what we had to do to survive.

Dealing meant we had a bed every night and food in our bellies growing up, but now it meant our futures were on hold.

Our boss, our former foster father, was a cruel man who only fostered us for a payday and servants to do his bidding. No matter how far we ran, he always lured us back. We were gluttons for punishment and greedy for money.

Coming from nothing meant when he dangled the money in our faces, we pounced like damn lions stalking their prey.

"How do you know it's the last one?" I asked as the club came into view in the distance. I didn't trust Bill, our boss. He was a vile man who crossed everyone and anyone when it was in his favor.

"He mentioned that there were some people sniffing around his ring." He lowered his voice, pulling out his pack of cigarettes and lighting another one.

"Who, Gray?" This man was like my brother. Most of the time, we were thick as thieves, but the other thirty percent of the time, I wanted to bash his face in for being so damn elusive. I hated when he played mind games. I was too old for that shit.

"Who do you think, East? The motherfucking cops, of course. They're on to him." We were only allowed in a small part of his drug ring. Bill didn't let anyone in on all the details. We were movers and nothing more. But I wasn't surprised the cops were onto him; it was only a matter of time.

I didn't say anything, mulling over the information. Tonight could be a setup. Gripping the blade harder as we neared the club, I eased a smile onto my lips and aimed it at the bouncer, slapping a fifty in his hand as we shook on an old arrangement. We'd been frequenting this club for years, and getting into a club when we were underage wasn't easy, so we paid him off. Now, years later, he let us in without a question, and we got to skip the line.

As we entered the dimly lit club, loud bass shook the ground, and bodies swayed to the explicit words bouncing off the walls. We eyed the crowd, looking for our targets.

Gray checked his phone, his face paling.

"I need to do this quickly. Anna isn't well. She thinks something is wrong with the baby. Can you take half the load?" We'd never done this, but like a fool, I nodded, and he extended his hand to shake, the packet dangling between his fingers.

"See you in an hour," I told him, and we parted ways with a

small nod, understanding in our eyes that we had to sell everything and get out of there.

I ordered a drink from the bar. Swirling the old-fashioned whiskey around in the glass, I surveyed the crowd. A group of barely-legal girls was clinging to guys that were far too old for them. When they came to the bar, I pretended to bump into one of the guys, like I'd seen Gray do a million times.

We started up an easy conversation, and then, I exchanged the pills for cash.

People screamed when guns were suddenly raised. The music lowered, and the lights brightened. "Hands up where I can see them!" I looked around for the best place to hide, and that was when I noticed the guns were pointed at *me*.

I caught Gray's eye behind the undercover cops. He mouthed a half-assed apology and ducked out, leaving me to take the fall by myself.

Raising my hands, the cash slipped from my fingertips and fluttered through the air until the bills fell to the floor. The silence was practically deafening.

My promising future was gone.

Chapter One

EASTON

Four Years Later

Life was lonely here, in a place where you couldn't trust your cellmate or even the guards, who were supposed to protect you. Just like my foster mother, who turned a blind eye every time *he* got mad at me and Gray for disobeying his orders.

I learned at a young age that I had to fend for myself. No one was going to protect me. No one was going to have my back. No one cared if I lived or died.

Begrudgingly, I sat down across from my lawyer. The cuffs bit into my skin as they secured me to the table, reminding me that even out of the cell in the presence of someone who believed my innocence, I was still a monster.

Rick, my attorney, crossed his arms over his big beer belly, glaring at the guard through two bushy, gray brows. His mustache moved with his lips, which turned into a scowl. "Is that necessary?" he grunted, and the guard shrugged.

"Protocol," came the guard's response before he lazily crossed the room and disappeared behind the door.

"I hate these fuckers," Rick grumbled, uncrossing his arms to fuss with the papers laid out across the table. "Now, I came with some good news. You're up for parole." I sat up, trying to read the mess of words before me.

"How the hell did we manage that?" I eagerly asked. When a frown appeared, furrowing not only his mouth but his brows as well, I leaned back and waited for the other half of the good news.

"Now, don't jump to conclusions. I ain't a magician boy." He put a pamphlet in my awaiting hands. "You will have to join this program to start the process."

Glancing at the letters in bold, I snorted.

PEN PAL OUTREACH PROGRAM

"This is a joke, right?" Rick shook his head, his double-chin wobbling.

"They want to see you take part in community events. This is for students at the local college. It's a requirement for them to graduate, and it will be a requirement for you to be released. I suggest you read the fine print. There are some other activities you will have to take part in here, and then, there's a program they want you to join once you're released."

I didn't care about the fine print. I wanted out.

"Where do I sign?"

* * *

DAYS PASSED without a letter from my pen pal, which was a little frustrating since I was relying on this person to get me out of here. They were supposed to reach out first. Rick assured me this was normal. I was at least assured when Rick informed me that my pen pal would only know my name and age. If I wanted to share my reasons for being arrested it was up to me.

"Looks like someone finally decided to take a chance on you." My least favorite guard threw the letter at me through the bars. I bit my tongue to keep my mouth shut. I longed for the day I could walk out of here, right past his smug face.

Scanning the envelope with my name written on it in perfect

script, my heart leaped. Someone wanted to talk to me. A complete stranger.

A stranger that needed to write to me to graduate.

Shaking the glimpse of happiness from my head, I glanced at the top left corner where the name Harley Cole was scripted with an address.

Who the hell named their child Harley?

Carefully opening the letter, I unfolded the single piece of paper.

*August 21*st

~~*Dear Easton,*~~
~~*Hi Easton,*~~
~~*Hey there,*~~
Hey,

Sorry for the mess above. They only give us one piece of paper, and I'm wasting it again. Just a heads up, I'm a terrible writer, but you know why I'm here. Ugh, that came off so rude. I'm sorry.

My name's Harley Cole, in case you didn't see the front of the envelope. My dad loves Harley Davidson, and my mom loves Harley Quinn, so it was within their mutual interest to give me the worst name possible. I bet you were wondering about that; everyone always asks, even though it's so rude.

Anyway, they told us to write about our lives, but I spend the majority of my day trying to run from it and stick my nose in a book. So, what do you do to ignore the reality of your life? Did that come off as rude? I didn't mean to be, I swear. I've just never spoken to someone in jail before.

I'm supposed to be a journalism major, but naturally, I can't think of a damn thing to write now. I don't care for the typical questions, but I guess I'll ask them anyway since it's expected.

1. *Your favorite color?*
2. *Your most hated color?*

3. *Your favorite childhood movie?*
4. *Your favorite TV show theme song?*
5. *Your favorite fast food?*
6. *Ketchup or mayo?*
7. *BMW or Mercedes?*
8. *Football or baseball?*
9. *Coke or Pepsi?*
10. *Chocolate or candy?*

Can't wait to hear back from you. Actually, no—can't wait to read back from you.
Your pen pal,
Harley

My lips curled into a grin of amusement. On paper, this girl was adorable as hell. Maybe this wouldn't be so bad. I liked this crazy girl.

She was so fucking *real*.

And a damn breath of fresh air.

Chapter Two

HARLEY

Tapping my pencil against the notepad, I glanced around my room, seeking inspiration. My professor knew creative writing wasn't my strong point. Yet he insisted on this assignment for my portfolio.

It had been three days since I sent my letter to the local prison, and every time I checked my mailbox, my heart sank with disappointment.

Easton had not written back.

Surely there was an incentive for him to be part of the program, too. I tried my best to make the letter engaging, but really, how creative could I be with one damn piece of paper? We weren't supposed to overwhelm them with the first one, but after that, all bets were off. Or so I was told.

My roommate, Kennedy, tapped obnoxiously on her phone, her long nails clicking with every word she typed out to her equally annoying boyfriend.

"Can you stop that?" she asked, her nasally voice piercing my ears.

"Can you stop texting?" I threw back, to which she just rolled her eyes, furrowed her blond brows, and sighed.

"Why do you always have the biggest stick up your ass?"

9

"Oh, I don't know, Kennedy." I sighed, throwing the notebook down on the bed. Sliding my feet into my sneakers, I stormed out of our small dorm. I stopped past the mailbox on my way out, hoping to see a letter, but was only greeted with an empty box. Just like all the days before. Ugh.

Taming my messy locks into a tight ponytail, I stretched quickly before tapping my smart watch and selecting the outdoor run option.

Running always made everything better.

An hour later, sweat was dripping down my hollow cheeks, and my heart was hammering against my chest. I sucked in greedy breaths of air as I stopped at the mailbox, surprised to see an envelope there.

My name was messily scrawled in black ink with Easton Diggs in the top left corner.

He finally answered me.

Kennedy was still lounging on her bed when I unlocked the door and breezed past her. She didn't even glance up long enough to stop texting.

Her straight platinum blonde hair was pulled back in a ponytail, tan legs on display with her tiny, barely-there shorts covering only what she deemed necessary.

She ate whatever she wanted, and still looked like a damn model. I wasn't as lucky.

When we moved in here, I thought we'd be friends, until she started spreading my secrets around campus.

She didn't have to tell everyone my secrets. And everyone started to hate the weird girl with two different colored eyes. I'd worn a contact for as long as I could remember to hide the fact that I was different.

But Kennedy couldn't keep it between us. And then, she'd told everyone about my parents, who never wanted to spend the holidays with me.

Secret after goddamn secret she shared with our peers, pushing me farther and farther away from making any friends.

Some days, I really hated her.

Flopping onto my bed, I ripped open the letter. Glancing at the top corner, I saw it was stamped with yesterday's date.

August 24th

Dear Harley,

Just thought I'd start out by letting you know that your name is killer. Wanna trade?

This one-piece-of-paper rule is bullshit, but what are we supposed to talk about that will fill more than one page?

I haven't written to anyone in so long, I had to remind myself how to hold a pen. My fingers already ache, but I'm going to do my best to answer all your questions.

I don't care why you're writing me. I haven't had any contact with the world aside from my lawyer, and he isn't the friendly type. You need to graduate, and I need to get out of here.

Everyone asks if I was born in the east, and honestly, I don't know where the name came from. I grew up in the foster system. My first memory is of a foster home. Names don't really bother me. They don't mean anything in the long run.

I like to read as well, but I've read all the books they have here, so I then switched to working out and trying to learn new hobbies. One of my previous cellmates was an artist, and he taught me how to draw, so that's what I do to ignore the reality of my life.

1. *Red*
2. *Yellow*
3. *Clifford, the Big Red Dog*
4. *Go, Diego, Go!*
5. *Sonic*
6. *Ketchup*
7. *BMW*
8. *Baseball*
9. *Coke*

10. *Chocolate*

Did I pass the test? Can't wait to read back from you, too. :)
Your pen pal,
East

My heart fluttered at the little smiley face. He passed the test with flying colors, alright. We had some of those things in common. Releasing the breath I didn't realize I was holding, my lips tipped into a smile. Maybe, there was someone for me to be friends with. Maybe this wouldn't be so bad.

"What has you smiling like an idiot?" Kennedy piped up, ruining the moment.

"Nothing you could possibly wrap your head around." She sighed with yet another eye roll. One day, they were going to get stuck in the back of her head, and I couldn't wait to witness it.

Folding the letter, I stuck it back in the envelope and pulled out my notebook, drafting the next one.

Chapter Three

EASTON

August 28th

East,

Were you born in the east? ;) Just kidding. Don't hate me. I couldn't help myself.

How are you? And none of that I'm good, how are you, bullshit. How are you really?

We might as well spill all our secrets. It's like a dear diary entry. It's not like you'll seek me out once you're released, right? Plus, I don't know a better way to get to know someone than through the skeletons in their closet. How many do you have?

I hate my roommate. I would rather live off campus in some shitty apartment building as long as I get away from her and her obnoxious boyfriend. Can you believe I naively thought we'd be instant friends? Until she spread all my secrets around campus, and then suddenly no one wanted to be my friend. This sounds like high school, but somehow it feels worse. Aren't we supposed to be adults now?

What about you? Do you have an annoying roommate? Kennedy and I are opposites. She'd rather be glued to her phone all day than pick up a book and read, which is absolutely horrifying.

Worst of all, she loves neon pink. How many twenty-two-year-olds do you know actually like neon pink?

You mentioned that you like to read. Thank God, we have something in common. What kind of books? I can send you some of my favorites, and we can have weekly book club discussions. Last week, I read The Great Gatsby. I really didn't understand all the hype. I watched the movie over the weekend and was disappointed as well. I hate when they make books into movies. Somehow, they always seem to be inadequate.

I figured you'd like to know my answers to the ten questions from last week. Surprise, surprise, we have a lot in common.

1. *Red*
2. *Neon pink*
3. *House of Mouse*
4. *Go, Diego, Go!*
5. *Does Red Robin count?*
6. *Ketchup*
7. *BMW*
8. *Baseball*
9. *Coke Zero*
10. *Chocolate*

Your turn to ask me ten. Can't wait to read back from you.
Your Pen Pal,
Harley

Chapter Four

HARLEY

August 31ˢᵗ

HARLEY QUINN,
   According to my paperwork, I was, in fact, born in the east. Not that I can be sure it's legitimate.
   I'm okay. The days blur together in here. Every day is the same, and I hate it the most. I sometimes forget I've been in here for four years, and I often wonder just how much the outside has changed.
   How are you really?
   Be careful. I might just come find you when this is all over and thank you for keeping me sane when all I want is to lose my damn mind. I never thought I'd actually look forward to a letter from a stranger. How deep are we going into the closet? I've got tons of skeletons, and not all of them are friendly.
   I hate your roommate, too. Pink hurts my eyes. I would rather live anywhere than here. I used to think my life was so terrible before, but I'd do anything to have it back. I have an annoying cellmate, but I guess that's life, right? I have to agree that books are king. What does she do all day on her phone? And for the record, I don't know any adults that like neon pink.
   I read anything I can get my hands on, and I know you're

wondering. I even read romance, but none of that straight sex shit. What do they call it—erotica? I need a good story to get lost in from the shit going on in my head. Book club sounds good. Haven't read The Great Gatsby. Send it over, and I'll pay you back in a year. I hate movies. They seem like a waste of my life. I'd rather be doing something. I have ADHD.

We do have a few things in common. Let's see if we have more.

1. *Can you ride a motorbike?*
2. *Can you drive a manual car?*
3. *Do you smoke?*
4. *If you had to eat the same dessert for the rest of your life, what would it be?*
5. *Convertible or sedan?*
6. *Are you a vegetarian?*
7. *Do your parents know you are writing letters to a prison inmate?*
8. *Marvel or DC?*
9. *Any tattoos?*
10. *What is your biggest fear?*

Until next week. Can't wait to read back from you.
Your Pen Pal,
East

Chapter Five
EASTON

September 6ᵗʰ

E*AST,*

Sometimes the days blur here, too, but nothing like what you are experiencing. I worry I may come off as insensitive to your situation, which is never my intention.

When was the last time you saw the outside world? I can try to inform you of all the major changes and keep you up to date for the next year.

I'm also okay. I could be better, but some days it's hard, you know? How are you this week?

I saw my parents this past weekend for Labor Day. It was a drag, as usual. They turned my room into a gym—can you believe it? I literally can't remember the last time I saw them use gym equipment, and they sure as hell didn't touch the treadmill or stupid cycle bike while I was there.

I know I've been gone for four years, but I kind of imagined they would wait until I officially moved out, you know? I had imagined living at home until my wedding night. But that's off the books now. Guess I really will be looking for a shitty apartment.

I look forward to your letters, too. Like check-my-mailbox-three-times-a-day excited. If you haven't been able to tell, I don't have many friends, if any, really. I don't even party. I'd rather be in bed reading a book.

Let's get lost in our closets. I'll share if you do.

Annoying roommate, annoying cellmate—dare I say we have more in common? She spends most of her time attempting to be an influencer on TikTok. Waste of time, if you ask me.

So, Mr. Diggs, you read romance? Your thoughts on Fifty Shades of Gray? Don't worry about paying me back. I'll go to the bookstore this weekend and find something exciting for us to read. We are totally starting with a romance. I hear there are some pretty spicy books out. What spice level do you like?

Can you take medication for your ADHD? My best friend in high school had ADHD, and the meds they put her on really helped her focus. She even decided to become a doctor because of it.

You have some very interesting questions. I hope I don't disappoint.

1. *My dad literally named me after Harley Davidson, so what do you think? Of course, I can.*
2. *Still learning that one. Spend most of the time fighting with my dad, so I barely see him. He was the one teaching me, so I stopped.*
3. *Not for me. My dad's a chain smoker, and I hate the smell. It makes me nauseous.*
4. *Vanilla ice cream. You can add any toppings, right?*
5. *Sedan.*
6. *I am a carnivore.*
7. *Yeah, they don't really care what I do. I already disappointed them by doing a journalism major. They were expecting something better.*
8. *Marvel. Is that even a real question?*
9. *None yet.*
10. *Dying without ever feeling 100% happy.*

You can write back sooner if you want.
Your favorite pen pal,
Harley Quinn

Chapter Six

HARLEY

September 8th

HARLEY QUINN, MY ONLY PEN PAL,

Say whatever you want; I don't think you're insensitive. It's not your fault I'm in here. Blame the system and the shitty person who was supposed to have my back.

I was arrested four years ago. Tell me everything there is to know.

Every day is a battle we have to overcome, some harder than others. I understand. I had a good day today. It started with your letter, and I wasn't letting anything ruin it. How are you?

When I read about your parents, I was almost grateful I don't have any. But I'm sorry they did that, too. You deserve better than that. I guess they want to try and find the motivation to work out with the equipment in the house?

Maybe you should talk to them? I'm sure they want you to stay with them as long as possible. I don't know—just trying to be helpful. From what I saw of my friends' parents growing up, they never wanted their kids to leave. I have housing lined up for me thankfully. My lawyer arranged it. Not that I'm terribly excited about *the area, but if you need a place in a year's time, I hear there's a spare room.*

I'll try to write more, but I can't make any promises. I have to wait on my guard to give me paper and a pen, and I'm only allowed to write when my cellmate is out, so there's no potential of me killing him or vice versa. Apparently, it's happened before.

I don't have any friends. I came to terms with being a loner. Even made rules to stay away from anyone that could potentially hurt me, but I'll break my rules for you.

Parties are overrated. I went to all of them in college. I have to believe there's more to life than that. But I guess I'll find out in a year.

What do you want to know, Quinn? How I got in here? If I've ever killed someone? Ask away, little bird.

What is an influencer? Who is she influencing? What the hell is TikTok? What has the world come to?

If you want to talk about romance, please don't waste my time with a poorly written book about sex. There was no plot in Ffity Shades, and Mr. Gray was and is a complete asshole who didn't know how to treat a woman. I promise you, there are men out there that know what they are doing.

What is a spice level?

I stay away from pills. They trigger too many memories from my past that I prefer to keep buried. Besides, I can usually keep it controlled if I stay active and keep my mind focused.

When was the last time you spoke to your best friend?

Your answers are about as interesting as my questions. I was hoping you'd be able to ride after what you said about your dad. My buddy taught me. I miss my bike the most. I miss the freedom of it. Manual transmissions really aren't that hard. I'll teach you when I get out, if you'd like. I have to agree with the smoking though. You passed my test.

Toppings are allowed—within reason. I'd have to go with chocolate cake. I can never get enough of it. Convertibles are a sin. Hello, fellow carnivore, what's your favorite?

From what I know, I think you're pretty great. I hope to meet you one day.

DC is king. I guess the friendship is over.

Just kidding.

I have a few tattoos. Any interest in ever getting one? I want to get more once I get out. It's true what they say—once you get one, it's addicting.

What would make you 100% happy? My biggest fear is falling in love.

What are the next ten questions?

Your only pen pal—I hope,

East

Chapter Seven

EASTON

EAST, MY ONLY PEN PAL,

Where should I start? I'm assuming you heard about when the world shut down for a year? How about the toilet paper shortage; did you hear about that, too? That's around the time TikTok popped up. Do you remember Vine? Kinda the same concept.

It started with six-second videos of dances, and now there's everything and anything on there. It's how I find the best books. Kennedy is a makeup influencer on there. She has a following of girls who idolize her and her obnoxious looks, her videos are a minute long, but she takes hours to create the look and then make the video. She even tries to enlist my help, and like the sucker I am, I hope every time, maybe just maybe she'll want to be friends.

I've held up a damn light long enough to know she'll only ever use me for her own gain.

Hmm, what else is there? Elon Musk bought Twitter. Do you know what Twitter is? I mean, you are old, right?

Oh, and the price for everything, and I do mean everything, skyrocketed.

I think that's everything of importance, if you don't count the war between Ukraine and Russia.

Today was a bad day for me. I haven't been able to keep any food down, but I won't get into details. How are you?

I tried talking to my parents about my living situation. They laughed and told me to grow up. Honestly, I don't know who they are anymore. I might need to take you up on that offer if you still like me in a year. Who knows—some of my skeletons might be too much.

I'd love to know the story of an inmate killing another with a pen. If you get any info on it, do share.

You'll break your rules for me? How sweet. You don't even know what I look like. For all you know, I'm ugly or weird looking. You should be careful, East. You can't trust anyone.

I don't need to know why you are in there; I don't care. I already know you aren't a murderer. Apparently, they don't let those inmates be part of the program.

Little bird?

Are you one of those men who know how to treat women? The ones out here in my classes can barely think past their other head, if you know what I mean.

Spice level is how hot you like your books. I'm in the three to four pepper range. They use the pepper emoji to rate it. You do know what emojis are, right?

I'm sorry about your medication, but hey, if you figured out a natural way to help yourself, even better. I don't like to take anything unless I'm about to die.

I spoke to my best friend about four years ago, so I guess we aren't really best friends anymore. :(

I will be taking you up on the manual lesson. I hate not knowing how. I'll let you ride my bike as payment.

Steak is my favorite meat. Is there really another superior option?

Don't make me blush, East. I'm okay. So far, you're the inter-

esting one. I'm just a nerd hiding away in her dorm. You're the elusive bad boy behind bars.

I'll get a tattoo one day, but it has to be for something or someone special. Maybe you can take me?

I don't know what true happiness is. Probably because I've never been 100% happy. There's always a darkness lingering in my mind. Some days, it's quiet enough to let me be, but other days, it paralyzes me.

Don't be afraid of love. I have to imagine it's the best part of being alive.

1. *Your eye color?*
2. *Dogs or cats?*
3. *Pizza or pasta?*
4. *Cars or bikes?*
5. *Coffee or tea?*
6. *Best memory?*
7. *Hair color?*
8. *Middle name?*
9. *Taylor Swift or Shania Twain?*
10. *Do you feel alone in there?*

Your favorite pen pal,
Harley Quinn

Chapter Eight

HARLEY

September 16th

September 16th

HARLEY QUINN,

Your letters get me through the day. I reread the old ones more times than I care to admit.

I did hear about the world shut down and the toilet paper short-age. Glad I missed out on that chaos. Yes, I do remember Vine, but I don't remember it ever being super popular.

I am not old, little bird. I am only twenty-six. I know what Twitter is and Facebook. Do you?

Is it a stomach bug? How are you now? I worry about you. I wish I could call you. I only ever talk to my attorney, and he's a boring old guy. But he's a good man who's been helping me pro bono.

I don't think your skeletons could ever be too much for me. Remember, I'm the one in prison.

I don't care what you look like. I know your heart is pure, which is all that matters to me. You're kind enough to take time out of your day to talk to me—some random creep in prison. You could be uglier than the Hunchback of Notre Dame, and I wouldn't care.

I don't trust anyone, but for some reason, I trust you.

You're my little bird because you are my freedom.

I've never had the opportunity to be that man. In college, I was too busy working to date, and I didn't want to involve anyone in my lifestyle choices. I'd like to think I would be the right man. I guess you'll be the judge of that by the end of our year.

Yes, little bird. I do know what an emoji is. How old did you think I was? Prehistoric?

Oh, and by the way, I have a thing for nerds, especially the kind that know how to ride bikes and eat steak. You're giving me a hard-on, Harley.

Are you blushing now?

I fight the same darkness. Remember, every day is a battle we must overcome. You aren't alone. When it seems to be too much, just think of me. Know if I could, I'd be there to help you through and show you the light.

1. *Blue*
2. *Dogs*
3. *Pizza*
4. *Both? I guess a car is more practical, but nothing screams freedom like a bike.*
5. *Coffee*
6. *Haven't had it yet.*
7. *Black*
8. *Ryder*
9. *Shania Twain*
10. *No, because I have you.*

Your only pen pal,
East

Chapter Nine

EASTON

EAST, MY ONLY PEN PAL,

Have I ever told you I hate the holidays? If not here is your disclaimer. Mom and Dad started to travel during my first year of college, so I end up either staying on campus like a loser or going home to an empty house.

Both options suck. Can you believe they actually went on a cruise the week of Thanksgiving? I guess they aren't grateful for me or really don't care what I do. Worst of all, there is no one else to spend the day of eating with. The rest of my family lives in New York, and because my parents left, they've shunned us. Mom's parents didn't approve of their marriage since Mom didn't choose an Italian man, so they eloped, and I've never met my grandparents or aunts and uncles. I guess I'm better off without them. At least Mom seems to think so. Doesn't mean I don't spend a lot of my time wondering.

What are your thoughts on the stupid holiday where we stuff our faces with too much food and pretend we are grateful for it and the people around us?

Christmas is usually worse because growing up, it was my favorite day of the year, even better than my birthday. My favorite

28

memories are of creeping down the stairs on Christmas Eve to check if Santa came. It sounds silly as I write it, but it's true.

They wouldn't let me send any food, so instead, here's one of my favorite romances. I know it's cliché. Try not to judge me. Dear John got me through a few rough patches growing up. One of those skeletons I'm still hiding, in case you're wondering.

I hope you enjoy it.

Do you get a decent meal? I hear the food is pretty good in there. Hopefully, you're eating better than me. I'm thinking of ramen noodles. I wish I wasn't alone over the holidays.

I wish you were here.

It's crazy that I've only known you for a month and haven't heard your voice or even seen you, but you're my best friend.

I'm counting down the days until your parole hearing. Only a few more months now, and then, you'll be stepping out of that hell and into another one, but hey you won't be alone anymore.

Do you think it will be weird when we see each other for the first time? What will we talk about? Will you like my voice? Will I like yours?

I think about it a lot, especially at night when I can't sleep.

Lately, you're the only thing on my mind.

Happy Thanksgiving, East.

Your favorite pen pal,

Little Bird aka Harley Quinn

Chapter Ten

HARLEY

December 30th

LITTLE BIRD,

I count down the days until I get to breathe fresh, uncontaminated air.

When my feet touch the concrete without the sound of metal clanking and my wrists are free.

I think about what it will feel like to be out of this wretched jumpsuit. How I long to wear a pair of sweatpants and a t-shirt.

In just a few months, you've reminded me that I do, in fact, have a purpose. You've given me something to look forward to each week and a happiness that I never thought I'd feel again.

I wish more than anything you didn't have to be alone tonight. I long to hold you, touch your skin, smell your perfume. I hate that your family leaves you. I hate that we're both alone and so far away from each other.

But I don't wish to change the past. If I wasn't here, we'd never have met, and although we still have a few more months to go, I am excited to start a new journey with you at my side.

I hate New Year's resolutions. The whole ideology of it irritates me. Especially those people who claim to start working out as their resolution. We all know if they really wanted to work out, they would have months ago.

Growing up, my resolutions were always the same. I longed to be adopted, and every year, I swore to myself I'd be better.

I'd smile brighter for my picture, I'd behave better, I'd be the perfect kid, and someone would want me.

And each year when no one wanted me, a piece of my heart, of my soul, shattered in oblivion.

I vowed never to make another one of those horrendous resolutions, but then you had to come along. You had to come in like a wrecking ball, and here I am breaking another rule. For you.

This year, I will meet you, and I will spend as many holidays as I can with you, little bird. We can be free together, to soar the skies and explore the world without a chain tugging us back.

Do you want that, too?

Am I crazy?

I arranged with my lawyer to have a phone call with you. He's going to reach out to you and coordinate a call. Only if you want.

If you only want to keep writing, then I'll be perfectly content with that.

Eight more months, little bird, and then I'll be free.

Happy New Year. Enjoy your last one alone because the rest are mine.

Your only pen pal,

East

Chapter Eleven

EASTON

A Few Months Later

August 15ᵗʰ

East, my favorite and only pen pal,
Can you believe this Friday you get out?
Are you sure you don't want a ride? You're only an hour away.
I'll gladly come meet you and bring you back to civilization.

To think we went from weekly letters to writing every few days, and then weekly phone calls. I don't want to be a stereotype. But when it comes to you, I can't help it.

I'm falling for you. The good girl falls for the inmate. My parents are going to love this, and I couldn't even give a rat's ass. You understand me in ways no one ever has. I can't wait for this weekend.

I think I'll know you the second I see you. Our souls were meant to find each other; of that, I'm sure. I'm afraid to speak the truth for fear that you'll run. Hell, Kennedy tells me I'm crazy at least ten times a day when I talk about you.

But I don't care.

I've put my heart on the line. It's out there, hanging in the breeze, waiting for you to claim or reject it.

If you want to remain friends and nothing more, I understand. It's kind of impossible and abnormal to fall for a stranger, don't you think?

In case you don't want to be only friends, and you want to be more, I'll be at The Rose on Saturday night at 7 P.M. as we agreed. And underneath my dress will be a surprise only for you.

I can't believe I just wrote that. Look what you've done to me, East.

And in what I'm hoping is a very rare chance, if this is the last time we speak, please know that I've loved writing you, and I treasure each and every letter you've ever sent me.

Your favorite pen pal,
Little bird

Chapter Twelve

EASTON

THE OLD, WORN-OUT, RIPPED JEANS FIT A LITTLE TOO snugly around my hips, and the black hoodie I'd been wearing that fateful day squeezed my biceps and chest, restricting my breath. But excitement coursed through my veins as I shoved my feet into my old, dusty sneakers, barely listening to Rick's speech about what I should and shouldn't do now that I was getting out.

I was so close to freedom, I could almost taste it. It was tantalizing. Addicting. It left my mouth tingling like the sensation I got when I ate something sweet after a long time.

I quickly signed the papers being pushed toward me by the elderly lady behind the desk, and her wrinkled lips tipped up into a small smile.

"I don't want to see you back here, and for heaven's sakes, get some new clothes." The grin that tore at my face was refreshing after years of hardly having any reason to smile.

"Will do." I glanced at her name tag. "It was nice to meet you, Fran." I turned to Rick, waiting with bated breath for what I was supposed to do now.

What was next? Did we step through those metal doors? Would the air be cleaner out there?

Was Harley thinking about me?

"Where is your head, Diggs?" Rick slapped a hand to my shoulder, startling me.

"Anywhere but here." He chuckled and nodded toward the doors.

Closing the small distance, my hand clasped the cold metal of the door handle, and I pulled it down, pushing the door open. Sunlight streamed into the room and washed over my face, blinding me in the best way possible.

One step onto the concrete, and then another, and another until the prison was behind me, and I was staring up into the big, blue sky, the sun beating down on my face, burning my skin.

"I'm free," I whispered.

The humid Summer air did nothing to deter my happiness as it stuck to my exposed skin. Sweat beaded at my hairline, and my hoodie became unbearably hot, but I took everything in.

"How does it feel, Diggs?" Rick was behind me. I could feel his presence at my back, but I didn't turn to look back at him, not wanting to see the hell I'd spent the last five years in.

"Better than I thought. It's everything I dreamed it would be and more."

"It's only going to get better from here, son. I promise your future is looking bright." He led me to a car that was waiting at the end of the street. We slid into the backseat, and the driver didn't even glance my way. He only addressed Rick, confirming a pin and then the address.

He then turned up the volume of the rock station playing through the speakers and pulled onto the road.

An hour later, we rolled to a stop on a quiet street. A big, gray apartment building loomed over us as the driver stopped the car and shifted it into park. He exited the vehicle and opened the door for Rick, then waited for me to slide out after him.

I nodded in thanks, but he adverted his gaze and hopped back into the small car, speeding off without a word to me.

Guess I was going to have to get used to that kind of treatment.

"What did I miss?" I turned to Rick, whose bushy brows were furrowed.

"Some people lost social skills after the quarantine. Don't mind him. Follow me and I'll show you your new home."

It was easy to forget a lot of people's lives had changed out here while mine had remained the same inside. But I also thought Rick was only making excuses for the man, not wanting to hurt my feelings.

After everything I'd been through, that was a hard thing to do. My feelings were no longer easily hurt.

Looking up at the building, I took notice of the fresh coat of paint, recently trimmed bushes, and the sharp scent of freshly cut grass permeating the air. It smelled like heaven compared to the concrete and sweaty male bodies I'd been smelling for the past five years.

We walked through a glass door, where a doorman greeted us with a head nod and smile. "Welcome, Mr. Diggs," the elderly gentleman greeted me, extending his hand.

I eyed him warily. Something wasn't adding up, and he seemed to notice the hesitation in my eyes because his lips curled into a warm smile.

Raising my hand to shake his, I shot Rick a worried look. He shook his head, dismissing me and then leading me away from the doorman, who was already greeting the next person. Why had he greeted me so warmly?

I followed Rick toward a set of gold elevators. He pressed the up button and checked his watch while tapping his shiny shoes on the marble floor.

"This place is..." I scratched my head, trying to find the right word. "Is this normal?" I asked instead, just as the elevator doors opened with a shrill beep.

We stepped into the elevator, and Rick pressed the button for the fourth floor. Just like that, we were whisked away. He fixed his suit jacket, eyeing the numbers as they crept up, avoiding my question.

"Rick, I can't afford this," I pointed out when the doors flew open again, and we stepped out onto the lush carpet.

"It comes with your job," he insisted, leading me to a dark gray door at the end of the hall, the number 404 printed in gold lettering on a plaque on the white wall. There was a keypad under the door handle, where Rick punched in four numbers and then twisted the handle, leading me inside my new home.

I was surprised to see it already decorated in grays and whites, much like the rest of the building. The appliances were state of the art, the furniture new, the floors clean, and the air crisp.

"What the hell is going on here?" I asked Rick, my eyes scanning over the open foyer that led into the kitchen. Along the one wall were three doors, all leading to carpeted bedrooms. Along the other wall were two doors, one hinting at a bathroom and the other a laundry room. "This isn't normal, man," I insisted, taking in the floor-to-ceiling windows that looked out onto a small park.

"Easton, it's part of your release. It comes with the job I secured. As long as you go to work every day and keep your record clean, it's yours with no expenses." I shook my head in disbelief.

Someone had to be playing a joke on me. I didn't deserve this.

"I need to go over some paperwork with you, and then I have to meet another client." He opened his briefcase and pulled out multiple documents, laying them out on the kitchen counter.

He pointed out the requirements of my release. The recommendation of giving back to the community. The contract for my new job.

I signed everything he laid before me, and soon, he was putting all the paperwork back in his briefcase and securing it. With a swift handshake, he was gone, leaving me in my shiny, new, expensive apartment that I felt out of place in.

Walking around the apartment, my fingers itched to write a letter. I missed Harley, my little bird. She'd become my best friend while I was in prison. Yet, I hadn't found the nerve to tell her about the reason I was in there. A fear remained in my heart that she would leave when she found out, just like everyone else before her. No one had ever stuck around, even before I got caught up in all the wrong things.

I wasn't ready to let my little bird go. Not when she gave me freedom in the first place.

* * *

THE MASTER BATHROOM was already stocked with the necessities, just like the fridge and kitchen cabinets. This was more than just a job offer; this was more than an ex-inmate deserved. And I wasn't sure why it was being offered to me.

I showered for the first time in five years as a free man. I let the hot water burn away my past sins and begged it to create a better man, one deserving of Harley.

I only had the clothes I'd worn home, a credit card in my old, battered wallet that had expired, and a few crumpled bills. It was enough to get me something decent to wear on Saturday night, but beyond that... I sighed.

After leaving the too-clean apartment, I entered the posh elevator and nearly crashed into an older lady, who clutched her skinny mutt to her chest and eyed me warily the entire four floors down.

I almost wanted to bare my teeth at her, become the animal she thought I was, but instead, I waited for her to exit the elevator and bid her farewells to the doorman. Then, she almost ran out of the lobby.

"She's skittish, that one," the doorman commented, holding the door open for me to exit.

"Apparently so. Are there any stores within walking distance?" He scratched his jaw, brows furrowing as he thought over my question.

"About two miles away, there's a shopping plaza, but it'll take you quite some time by foot. Can I order you an Uber, sir?" Sticking my hands in the pockets of my jeans, I shook my head.

"No, thanks. I like to walk. Gives me time to think. Will you be here later, Mister..."

"Sherman. Just Sherman, sir. Enjoy the walk. Luckily for you, no storms are predicted today. I will be here until dusk, and then John starts his shift. He'll be here until dawn." I nodded, taking in the information, and then murmured my own goodbye as he held the glass door open.

I followed his directions, the summer sun sweltering as it beat down on my back. Sweat rolled down my hairline, soaking the neckline of my shirt.

But like I admitted to Sherman, walking was peaceful with the song of birds singing in the distance, the rare brush of the sticky breeze, and a passing car whizzing by every few minutes.

My mind drifted to the same place it had been swimming for the last year—Harley.

What would she look like?

What color were her eyes?

Would she find me attractive?

Would she flee?

Would she be at the bar tomorrow night?

What would she think of me?

What was she going to wear under her dress?

Would she want to kiss me?

What would she taste like?

What would she feel like beneath my fingers?

"Watch it!" a woman's voice shook me from my thoughts as she collided into me, bags dangling off her arms.

"Sorry, ma'am. Didn't see you." I raised my hands defensively.

"Well, open your damn eyes!" she huffed and turned, barely giving me a glance. Shaking my head, I looked up. Spotting a thrift store sign, I headed in.

Scanning the aisles, I found a pair of jeans and a button-down shirt. They were good enough for a bar on a Saturday night.

Then, I picked up a few more items and checked out, handing over all the cash in my wallet.

Thankfully, I started my new job on Monday, but all I could think about was tomorrow night. I knew the moment my eyes landed on her, I would just *know*. I didn't have to see a picture of Harley to know what she looked like.

I'd know my little bird in a crowd full of people.

Chapter Thirteen

HARLEY

I PACED THE CONFINES OF MY DORM ROOM, TUGGING AT the wet strands of my hair, barely containing my nerves for tonight.

I was going to meet Easton, the inmate I'd been writing letters to for the last year, later this evening. He was the only person on this planet that I had trusted with most of my secrets and the only friend I had.

What if something went wrong?

"Do you mind? You're going to mess up the rug I just bought," Kennedy commented from her bed, where she was busy making yet another TikTok with some crazy makeup look she'd invented this morning.

She was the last person I wanted to ask but the only girl I spoke to on campus and, unfortunately, my only hope.

"Can you help me? I have a date tonight, and..." She tapped at her phone and sprung off the bed with a squeal.

"You have a date? What do you need? Of course, I'll do your makeup." I inched away from her, wary of the sudden kindness she was showing me.

"Are you sure?" I asked, and she nodded.

"I know we haven't gotten along, but I love doing makeup, and I can post a picture of the look on my Instagram."

Of course, she would help me, but only if it benefited her. I honestly shouldn't have expected anything different.

"Right. Okay, well, I just need to go find something to wear, and then we can get started." She settled back down on her bed.

"Where are you going and with who?" she nosily asked, looking at her own reflection in the small makeup mirror she had on the bed.

"The new bar downtown—The Rose. Is it any good?" I avoided answering her about Easton. He had been mine, and only mine, for the last year, and the thought of sharing him with Kennedy was too much to bear.

"Oh, yeah. It's great. So, you forgot to mention the who?" she pressed again, applying pink eyeliner to her one eyelid.

"An old friend." I pulled a brush through my wet hair and quickly grabbed my bag and shoes, exiting the room before she could ask any more questions I wasn't ready to answer.

I never liked to go shopping. I hated trying on clothes, only to be disappointed when they didn't fit. Parking at the mall, I walked across the asphalt, the summer rays beating down harshly on my exposed skin, the humidity weighing me down a little more with each step until I entered the airconditioned building and sighed with relief.

I stopped first at one of the biggest department stores and found myself looking at dresses I knew would never fit. But I couldn't seem to tear my eyes from a red one in particular. Grabbing it in three sizes, I prayed one of them fit. I didn't care which one it was, so long as it was flattering.

Thankfully, the medium fit. It was a little snug around my hips, but as long as I didn't eat for the rest of the day, it would be perfect. I purchased the tight, strapless dress, and then headed to the lingerie department.

I had promised East a present.

God, I prayed he was good-looking and not one of those guys

covered in face tattoos with long, slimy hair. I only hoped I was making the right decision by meeting him tonight.

After picking a matching, strapless red lace bra and thong, I left the store, cheeks flaming the entire walk to my car.

I skipped lunch, only drinking a bottle of water to fill my growling stomach. I'd been battling my weight for as long as I could remember and skipping meals helped. It was a better alternative to eating and then throwing up after.

Stopping at the campus gym, I ran on the treadmill for thirty minutes before rushing back to the dorm. Kennedy was now washing her face of the insane makeup look, chatting away to her boyfriend on the phone about their evening plans when I entered the small space.

She didn't acknowledge me when I dumped my bags on the bed and slid into our bathroom. The best part of not dating was the lack of shaving I had to do for the last few years. Spending a long time under the hot spray of the low-pressure shower head, I scrubbed my skin with my favorite vanilla body wash and shaved everywhere.

Thirty minutes later, Kennedy was banging on the door. "Hurry up, Harley! I need to do your makeup. I have plans later with Aaron," she hollered through the door.

Drying off, I brushed my teeth, applied my moisturizer, and put in one blue contact, hiding my one green eye.

I'd spent the majority of my childhood being told I was special to have two different colored eyes. But at the start of middle school, that turned into bullying, and by high school, I begged my parents to hide my birth defect.

There was no way I was letting East in on all my secrets just yet. For all I knew, he'd lied about his or hadn't told me the worst ones, and tonight, I wanted to be normal. I wanted to be pretty like all the other women in the bar. I didn't want to stand out for being different.

Emerging from the bathroom, I saw Kennedy had already laid out all her products on the small desk area we shared. "What are you wearing tonight?" she asked, putting her phone down and standing from her bed.

I showed her the red dress and then darted back into the bathroom to change into the matching lingerie and dress. After twisting my hair on the top of my head with a claw clip I exited and sat down at the desk, where Kennedy spent the next hour transforming me into someone pretty.

"Well, fuck, you look good, if I do say so myself," she commented after taking my dark hair out of the clip and straightening it. She moved a few strands over my shoulders, sprayed something on my face, and then started snapping pictures with her phone.

I hadn't seen my face yet and prayed she hadn't turned this random act of kindness into a tragedy.

"Okay, go look." I stood, pulling down the dress as it rode up my legs, and slowly walked into the bathroom, terrified.

Flipping the light on, Kennedy stood behind me, arms crossed over her chest, nodding impatiently for me to look in the mirror.

Holding my breath, I turned to look at my reflection and gasped.

I had never looked this beautiful in my life. She'd enhanced all my features, hid my god-awful freckles, and made my eyes and lips look bewitching.

"Kennedy, wow, thank you," I whispered, blinking slowly. The fake lashes she'd glued on fluttered across the top of my eyelids, making my eyes appear bigger and more alluring.

"Of course. It was fun. I never get to practice on anyone that isn't me." She shrugged and exited the bathroom. Stealing another long glance in the mirror, I sprayed some perfume on and found her cleaning up the desk when I exited.

Wrapping my arms around her, she stiffened, but I was so overcome with emotion, I didn't care for once.

"Kennedy really, this is a dream. I've never looked like this before." She blushed, a hint of a smile tugging at her lips.

"You are beautiful without makeup, Harley." She hugged me

back and then looked over at my pile of shoes in the corner of the room. "Did you buy shoes to wear tonight?"

Shit. I had forgotten.

She must have seen the panic in my eyes because she quickly rushed over to her side and pulled out a pair of black stilettos.

"Try these."

I never wanted this version of Kennedy to leave. This was someone I could be friends with. This was someone who cared if I looked good for a date and not the girl who spilled all my secrets.

Slipping the heels on, they were a little tight, but she assured me they would loosen the more I walked, and then she was pushing me out of the dorm and promising to catch up tomorrow.

In my car, I nervously drummed my fingers on the steering wheel, following the GPS to the bar downtown.

I tried to play some songs to boost my courage, but by the time I parked my car, I could barely string a sentence together without my tongue feeling heavy.

I managed to get a barstool at the already crowded bar and ordered a drink just like Kennedy suggested. Sipping the martini, I eyed the room.

Was he here?

How would I know he was the one?

Would he like what he saw?

Would he still want me after seeing what I looked like?

I downed the martini and ordered another from the bartender, my fingers shaking as they curled around the glass. Bringing it to my lips, I took a long sip.

The cool liquid was numbing my nerves a little more with every minute that passed, and as I watched the dimly lit room, I assessed every man, waiting for the one.

Checking the time on my phone, I noticed it was five minutes past the agreed meeting time, and a slither of fear entered my mind. Maybe he wasn't coming.

Another five minutes passed, and I slammed the empty

martini glass to the bar and stood on shaky legs, almost losing my footing as the effects of both drinks slammed into me at once.

I really should have eaten something earlier.

Looking down at my feet I focused on the floor in front of me, needing to get to the safety of my car.

Bumping into a firm shoulder, I tripped over my damn feet and started to sway to the side, regretting the stilettos I had no business wearing. I should have stuck with sneakers.

A warm hand latched onto my arm, steadying me, and I was forced to look into the most beautiful eyes I'd ever seen. Blue eyes, clearer than the Caribbean, pierced mine, and I forgot how to breathe as my heart fluttered wildly in my chest.

"And you, my little bird," he murmured. "Where do you think you're going?" His deep voice washed over me, and I blinked slowly. *It was him.*

Easton.

God had blessed me with the most beautiful man I'd ever laid my eyes on, and I was speechless.

Chapter Fourteen

EASTON

I HADN'T KNOWN WHAT TO EXPECT WHEN LOOKING FOR Harley. She'd given me one clue to find her in a bar full of women. The Rose was dimly lit with carpeted floors, dark gray walls, and roses twined around dark chandeliers just out of reach. Music thrummed through the space, fighting the loud chatter of drunk customers that swayed to its hypnotizing notes.

Scanning the few tables, all the women in red were draped over men, and none held my interest longer than a fleeting second.

And then, I saw her.

Dark, almost black, hair hung like fine silk down her back, hiding delicate shoulders that moved with a sigh as she slammed her martini glass down on the bar. She stood quickly, getting the attention of the man beside her, who also stood and reached for her.

I moved quickly through the crowd, needing to get to my little bird before she fled. Watching her every move, I saw a small scowl turn her red lips down, and her long lashes fanned her face as she glanced at the floor before taking an uncertain step forward. In slow motion, she wobbled, fear flashing in her blue eyes. Wrapping my fingers around her forearm, her muscle tensed, and her head snapped up to look at me.

47

Instantly, I was struck by her beauty.

The scowl dropped, and a soft noise of surprise escaped her parted lips. Her blue eyes scanned my face, growing wide as they swept over my body.

"And you, my little bird—where do you think you're going?" I swallowed past the lump in my throat. It was really her. She was real.

And fucking stunning.

She blinked slowly, her dark brows furrowing. The spicy scent of her perfume invaded my senses as she stepped closer to me. I focused on her eyes, then her small nose, her flushed cheeks, and her bow lips.

I had dreamed about her for months, and she never came close to anything I could have imagined. I wanted to kiss her. Ruin her perfect, red lips. I wanted her hands around my neck, nails digging into my skin.

I wanted every man in the bar to know she was my little bird.

"East?" Her voice shook. Fear laced her tone, and I fell in love with the way my name sounded coming from her lips.

"It's me." I stepped into her, our toes touching, chests brushing, hearts beating faster than the wings of a hummingbird. She raised a hand to my cheek, her touch soft, gentle.

Perfect.

"I thought you weren't coming. I was going to leave," she whispered, closing her eyes and sighing. "I am so nervous."

"Me, too. I wasn't expecting the prettiest woman in the room to be waiting for me tonight. God, Harley, tell me what I did to deserve meeting an angel?" She giggled, her head shaking.

"I don't care about your past, East." Somehow, she always knew what to say. The same way every letter saved a piece of my soul on my worst days. "Please kiss me." Her words were a whisper against my jaw, her breath hot against my neck. The hand on my cheek slid into my short hair, and I groaned.

"How much have you had to drink?" Closing my eyes, I

wished I couldn't smell the alcohol on her breath. In moments like these, I wished I didn't have a conscious.

"Not enough. Don't make me beg, East. I've waited long enough." She pressed her chest to mine. My hands ached to touch her, to peel the tight, red dress from her soft, pale skin. Cupping her firm butt, I held her to me, and my other hand slid into her thick hair. She moaned.

"I want you to remember this in the morning without regrets, my little bird." My words came out on a rasp, desire rippling through my body, tensing my muscles.

"I'll never forget this. I want you."

Closing the remaining distance, unable to resist her a moment longer, I brushed my lips to hers. They parted with a soft sigh, her body curling into mine. The hand in my hair clenched, and I pulled her tighter against me as my tongue traced the seam of her full, bottom lip. A little noise of desire ripped from her throat.

Nibbling her bottom lip, I chased the sting away with my tongue and sought entrance to her warm mouth, my one hand kneading her butt, the other clutching at her desperately.

She turned her face from mine, sucking in a greedy breath of air. I continued peppering kisses along her jaw, tasting her sweet skin, hearing her moans, and needing more than a brief moment of ecstasy in a bar surrounded by strangers.

I sucked on the delicate skin below her ear, bruising her skin with a bite of desire. Then, I nibbled on her earlobe as she mewled in delight, her body flush against mine.

"More, East. I need more," she begged, her lips brushed the shell of my ear. A shiver of desire skated down my spine.

"I'll give you whatever you need, my little bird."

I turned my head, seeking her lips and stealing her breath once more, inhaling her gasp of surprise when I bit down hard on her lip.

"Take me home," she requested against my lips, kissing the corner of my mouth. Pulling away from her, I looked over her flushed cheeks, dilated eyes, and swollen lips.

"Are you sure?" she nodded, and I smoothed a hand down her hair and then wiped at her smeared red lipstick. She did the same to my face, but from one glance at the people around us, there was no hope in fixing our disheveled state.

Everyone already knew where the night was headed for us.

She slipped her hand into mine, her small hand cold, as she followed me out the bar and into the humid, night air.

"I don't have a car. We'll have to walk." I looked over her tight, red dress and heels.

"I have one, but I can't drive." She laughed, swaying on her feet. Stepping into me, she leaned her head on my shoulder. "Can you?"

I nodded, and she led me to an old, black BMW. Once she was safely strapped into the passenger seat, I rounded the hood, checking our surroundings before backing out of the parking lot and merging onto the busy street.

"Do you have any food at your place?" she slurred, holding her head up with her hand, leaning against the door for support. "I'm so hungry. I couldn't eat all day."

Reaching across the small, center console, I rested my hand on her thigh. "How about some pizza? I'm starving." She had to be as nervous as I was to not have eaten anything.

"That sounds like a good idea," she mumbled, closing her eyes, her long lashes brushing her high cheekbones. "Can we eat at your place? I don't want to stand anymore. I hate these stupid shoes. They were Kennedy's idea," she rambles on, talking about how her roommate helped her get ready for tonight. The same roommate I thought she hated.

"I've got a frozen one at the apartment." I couldn't bring myself to call it home, I hated the foreign word. Home had been a jail cell, and before that, it had been my car. Home was a reminder of everything I could never have, and now, I had a place to call mine, but nothing felt right about the luxurious apartment.

Navigating through the dark streets, lit only by dim streetlights, I glanced at her every few minutes, watching her fall asleep, her chest rising and falling with deep, even breaths.

Parking her car in my designated spot in the parking garage, I shut the car off and surveyed the full lot of expensive cars.

I didn't belong here.

Shaking that thought off, I exited the driver's side and walked around the back of the car, fighting a grin at the small, pink sticker in her rear window that read, *You just got passed by a girl.*

Carefully opening the door, I squatted and released her seatbelt, gently shaking her arm to wake her. She blinked slowly, her eyes coming into focus as she assessed her surroundings.

"Sorry." She blushed, and I stood, offering her my hand as she stepped out of the car. Wobbling on the sexy shoes, she took my offered support and rested her other hand on my chest. "You're sweeter than I imagined," she whispered, threading her fingers with mine and following me through the lot to the elevator.

We stood in the metal box as it raced to the lobby, and I was struck by her simple words. *What had she been expecting? Who was I supposed to be?*

"It's only for you, little bird."

"You're not what I expected." She leaned on me as we exited the elevator and walked across the lobby to the elevator that would take us to my apartment. The nighttime clerk, John, waved from his desk, and I nodded in acknowledgment.

"What were you expecting?" I asked as we waited for the elevator. She looked up at me and then at the grand lobby over my shoulder.

"Didn't expect you to have money, for starters." She gestured behind us.

I was waiting for that comment. "Anything else?"

"*Hmm.* Don't take this the wrong way, but no visible scars." Her eyes skimmed over my face and exposed skin.

"And where would I have gotten those?" She blushed, but I saw where her mind was going. "I didn't get in any fights," I assured her. "It's not my scene."

"I know you have tattoos, but I can't see them." We stepped into the elevator, and the doors closed once I pressed my floor. Slowly, we began our ascent.

"Were you expecting them on my neck and face?" Her blush deepened as she leaned against the wall of the elevator.

"Maybe. You're not fitting any of the stereotypes." The cab came to a stop, and the doors opened. I extended my hand to her, leading her to my apartment door where I typed in the code to unlock the door.

She made a little noise of surprise as she took in the lavish apartment, her big, blue eyes darting over the couch, kitchen, and big windows that overlooked the park right behind the building and the rest of the city beyond.

I kicked off my shoes at the door and then kneeled to unstrap her heels. She crouched with me, pushing my hands aside. "You don't have to do that." Silently, I gently brushed her hands to the side and continued untying the thin strap around her ankle.

"Please," I murmured when she frowned at me. She stood and let me take off her right shoe. I caressed the arch of her cold foot, kneading the sore muscles, and she sighed. I repeated the action with her left and then stood, pressing a quick kiss to her lips before leading her into the kitchen.

She slid onto a barstool, holding her head up with both hands as she watched me. I found the frozen pizza I'd seen earlier and turned the oven on. At that moment, I was thankful the place came stocked with food, dishes, and appliances. I wouldn't be here with her now if it didn't.

Once the oven had heated up, I slid the pizza in and turned back to the fridge. "Water?" She shook her head.

"I'm not ready."

"Not ready for what?"

"To wake up from this dream." Rounding the counter, I stood in front of her. Sliding both my hands into her thick, silky hair, I made her look at me. My thumb traced her bottom lip, pulling it from between her teeth.

"It's not a dream, Harley. I'm real. We're real. This is real."
She nodded, her eyes glazing over with lust.

"Don't make me beg, East. I hate begging for what I want."

"Tell me what you want, Harley. I can't read your mind, little
bird." I brushed my nose to hers, inhaling her sweet scent. A trace
of alcohol lingered in the air between us, and I knew it was
clouding her judgment, reminding me that I needed her to eat so
she could sober up a bit. But I wanted her to beg for me. For us.

"You. I want you." Her lips ghosted over mine, teasing and
testing my patience all at once.

"Where do you want me?" I nipped at her bottom lip,
devouring her moan.

"Everywhere, Easton. I don't just want you; I *need* you everywhere." My little bird was begging.

And it was snapping my restraint.

Chapter Fifteen

HARLEY

"WHERE DO YOU WANT ME?" HIS VOICE WAS RASPY AND full of desire, sending a chill down my spine as he nipped my bottom lip, teeth sinking into the sensitive flesh.

"Everywhere, Easton. I don't just want you; I *need* you everywhere," I begged in a whisper, pushing my breasts against his chest, needing to relieve the burning ache that thrummed through my entire body. I needed him to soothe the burn with his touch and his alone.

His hands cradled my face, fingers sinking into my hair, tightening his grip on me, I wanted to weep with relief, but as he took my mouth in a searing kiss, fireworks exploded behind my closed eyes, and my body came alive beneath his touch.

His lips, his touch, his heat—everything that was Easton sent my mind into overdrive. Warmth pooled between my thighs, and desire for this beautiful man invaded every single one of my senses.

The brief moment was over when the oven's buzzer blared, jolting us apart. I was cold without his hot hands on me and his body pressed to mine. He shook his head, taking a step away from me and towards the oven.

He opened the oven and reached in before I noticed his bare hands.

"Wait!" I jumped off the bar stool, knocking it over in my haste, and he stopped, turning to look at me in confusion. "Your hands." I pulled open all the kitchen drawers until I found a pair of oven mitts and handed them to him.

He shook his head again and then placed the sizzling pizza onto the cool, marble counter. He dropped the mitts and gripped the counter. Dropping his head, he groaned.

"You are driving me fucking wild, Harley." His voice was low, desire rippling through every word.

I wrapped both arms around his middle. Pressing my cheek to his broad back, I inhaled a shaky breath. Wordlessly working the buttons of his shirt with my fingers, I slowly undid each one until the shirt was hanging open and loose, and I trailed my hands up his arms, over his shoulders, pushing the shirt off until it dropped to the cool tile beneath my bare feet.

I slipped in front of him. His tan skin was covered in goose-bumps, and he shuddered when I traced the first tattoo that caught my attention.

The black snake on his collarbone almost looked real, slithering through his skin, protecting him from evil. I touched it softly, and he sighed, his fingers regripping the counter, this time harder, the muscles in his biceps and shoulders bunching with his strength.

"Why a snake?" I whispered. Stepping onto my tiptoes, I leaned forward and brushed my lips to the intricate woven skin ink, and he groaned.

"It's a symbol of virility, rebirth, and wisdom," he stuttered when I traced my lips and tongue over the small snake.

"Virility for strength?" I whispered against his heated skin.

He looked down at me, the heated look in his hooded eyes causing a whole swarm of butterflies to take flight in my stomach.

"Among other things." He grinned and dropped his hands, resting them on my hips, fingers digging into my skin through the thin material of my dress. "It also means a strong sex drive." He winked at my gasp and flushed cheeks. "Don't worry, baby. It's a good thing for you."

I swallowed, my eyes darting between his ocean-blue ones and his lips.

"Rebirth?" I tried to sort through my muddled thoughts and focused again on the tattoo.

"You have a lot of questions, little bird." He dropped his head a little, and his lips skimmed my jawline, his hot tongue tasting my skin. "When I was first arrested, I was devastated, couldn't believe my best friend could betray me, so I decided to change. I wasn't going to be the orphan boy anymore."

"Wisdom?"

"I won't repeat the same mistakes again. I know better than to trust the first person to show me love and safety."

I dropped my forehead to his bare chest, inhaling the scent of his skin. I had so much to learn about him, so many walls to climb if I was ever to win this beautiful man over and make him truly mine.

"You need to eat before the food gets cold," he mumbled into my hair, but I didn't want to move. I didn't want another moment to end prematurely.

He gently pushed me back, but I leaned further into him. "No," I mumbled into his skin, and he froze. "I'm not ready."

"Ready for what, Harley?"

"For this moment to end." His arms slid tightly around me, and I tried to memorize this moment, his strength wrapping around me, the smell of his cologne, the gentle rise and fall of his chest beneath my cheek. Everything about this moment was perfect.

When I found the courage to move away a few minutes later, he found two plates for us and cut the pizza into triangles. He said nothing as I stared at his back, covered in small, scattered circular scars of burnt flesh.

I covered my mouth, trying to prevent the gasp from escaping, but obviously, he heard because he tensed.

"You were right about scars," he muttered, dishing up two slices each and then turning to me with the plate extended in a shaky hand.

"East..." I took the plate, my fingers brushing his, and he flinched, breaking my heart.

"My foster dad didn't like it when I disobeyed him," he shrugged, "but he sure did like to smoke, and more than that, he loved to use me to put out his cigarettes."

I hated the truth of his past. I hated the scars he carried and the armor that he wore like a second skin because of the evil he endured.

He leaned against the counter and slowly ate his pizza, but I struggled to lift the warm food to my mouth. I was too nauseous from his admission to eat.

Regardless, I took a small bite. Chewing slowly, I watched him. His eyes were on the floor, no longer on me, and I swallowed the food.

Time passed agonizingly slow as we both ate the pizza in silence. I was hungrier than I thought, but I could barely swallow each bite.

He finished the rest of the pizza and then placed his plate in the dishwasher. I put mine in beside his and helped clean the kitchen. Once we were done, he took my hand and silently led me to the couch in the center of his apartment. He flipped off the kitchen lights on his way, bathing us in only the moonlight that streamed in through the big floor-to-ceiling windows.

He settled into the middle of the couch, pulling me on top of him, my thighs straddling his lap as he cradled my face in his big hands.

"You are so fucking beautiful, Harley. Your eyes are my fucking kryptonite." He leaned up to press a quick kiss to my lips, and my eyes fluttered closed in relief.

The night wasn't over.

The buzz from my two martinis was long gone. The confidence they brought was slipping away with every minute that passed, and for just a fleeting moment, I wondered if this was the best idea.

Was I really going to sleep with a stranger?

What would Kennedy say if she knew I was going to have sex with a recent inmate?

What would my parents say?

Would they care?

Did I care?

"Where are you, little bird?" Easton's blue eyes were laser-focused on me. And regret flooded me as I looked at him. Insecurity flashed through his eyes. He was a broken man trying to give me a piece of himself.

"Here. I'm here."

"Things change when alcohol isn't flowing, huh?" He whispered like he could read my mind, and I hated it.

Rolling my hips against his hard erection, he groaned, and I whimpered at the contact. I wanted him.

"No. The voices just get louder. Make them go away, Easton, please." I leaned forward, squeezing my thighs around his.

"Your wish is my command, baby. You want them to be quiet? I'll make them fucking silent." He closed the space between us, stealing my lips in another searing kiss, sucking my soul straight from my body.

Somehow, he always understood, even on just a piece of paper.

And I didn't care what anyone said or thought. Easton was the only one who mattered now. My hands slid up his neck and into his short hair, and I pulled him to me. He groaned into my mouth and nipped at my bottom lip.

"Bed."

One word and he stood, his hands sliding beneath my butt, holding me to him. His lips left mine to trail kisses across my jawline to my neck. I held onto him, amazed at his strength, and when he threw me down on a plush mattress, a nervous giggle bubbled from my chest.

His eyes swept over me. Moonlight cast us in a soft glow as he towered over me. He undid his belt and then slid down the zipper of his pants, his eyes never leaving mine. I was shaking with desperation for his calloused hands to trail over my skin, to leave me burning with the rough sensation that was all him.

I wanted his hands on my skin. I was desperate for it.

His pants fell to the floor, revealing black boxer briefs that left very little to the imagination. His thick erection was pressing against the silky-looking fabric, desperate to be freed. My breath hitched in my throat.

He crawled onto the edge of the bed and slowly made his way over my body, dropping a kiss to my calf and then my thigh before pushing the edge of my tight dress up.

"You're the best fucking present, my little bird." He nipped at the skin he just exposed and then chased the sting away with a soft kiss.

I squirmed beneath him, reaching for him. "Please, East," I begged, not even sure what the hell I wanted more: to be kissed or to be undressed by him.

"I need to get this damn dress off," he mumbled. Sitting up, he slid his hands beneath my back and pulled me up, my dress moving with me. My skin pebbled as his fingers grazed my thighs. He groaned at the sight of my red lace thong and then swore at the string that connected them to my lace bra. "Fuck, Harley. You're fucking killing me, little bird."

He threw my dress behind him and laid me on the bed.

"You kept your promise." He skimmed a hand over my quivering torso, cupping my breast. I moaned into the heated air.

"East..." I waited for him to rip the flimsy material from my body, but instead, he crawled over me, his nose skimming my skin, his lips leaving a blazing trail of desire. He dropped his mouth to the curve of my neck and placed a gentle kiss there. "What are you doing?" I felt his smile against my skin.

"Treating you how you deserve."

Heat flooded my entire body at the rasp in his voice, and I pulled his mouth to mine, needing more.

"I need you, East. I need you now."

"You'll have me, baby. You'll have me all fucking night long." He winked, a cocky grin taking over his features. I was positive I was about to combust from suspense alone. Pushing him up, I let my eyes skim over the few tattoos on his chest and biceps, the ridges of his stomach, and further down until my breath caught in my throat.

I swallowed as my mouth filled with saliva, and my gaze took in every dip and valley before slowly rising to meet his heated look.

Easton's cocky grin was replaced with hunger. His eyes were wide as his tongue darted out to lick his lips. He wanted to devour me, and I wanted nothing more than to let him.

I gripped the thin material of my thong and started pushing down, but his hands caught mine.

"You're mine to unwrap, Harley. Don't take that away from me." He wrapped two fingers around the string connecting my bra and thong. Snapping it, he slowly dragged my thong down my legs. Heat pooled between my thighs at the hunger in his gaze.

When I rubbed my thighs together to bring myself some relief, he shook his head.

"Be patient, my little bird," he whispered, throwing the thong behind him. He hovered over me, his hands on either side of my head as he held his heavy weight just a breath away from my body. His thick length brushed against my quivering heat, and my moan bounced off the walls.

God, it had been so long.

I couldn't remember the last time someone made me feel like this.

"I'm never going to get used to this," East groaned in the back of his throat, eyes devouring every inch of me on display for him.

He dropped his head to the crook of my neck, growling as my breasts held him up.

I closed my eyes, my body alive with anticipation. He pressed his body against mine, his heat searing my skin.

"Take it all off," I whispered, my own voice thick with desire.

"I want to take it in," he mumbled, kissing the valley between my heavy breasts.

"Please." I reached for the front buckle on my bra, but he used one hand to push me away and snapped open the red lace.

"I don't fucking deserve you, Harley." His voice was thick and raspy.

His fingers gently brushed across my skin, kneading my aching breast. My heart stuttered at his tender touch, and I met his gaze, full of unsaid emotion.

I placed my hand over his chest, his heart beating a rhythm that matched my own. Two hummingbirds trying to stay aflight.

"*East.*" It came out as a plea for more.

My nails dug into his shoulders, pulling a groan from him. "I can't be gentle with you."

"I don't want gentle. I just want you."

His eyes were liquid with heat, and his hand tracked down my hot skin, cupping my ass, while the other remained by my head, holding himself above me. I pressed my lips to his, letting him take the lead, owning my mouth and murmuring his dirty desires against my lips.

I wanted him to take what he needed from me. He'd been a prisoner for five years. Five years of wanting someone to fulfill his needs, but more importantly, he'd spent his entire life waiting for someone to love him.

I'd love him with everything I had, and right now, I had my body, something he so desired and needed.

He broke away from the kiss, and his chest rubbed against my breasts as we both tried to catch our breaths.

We both groaned when he slipped his fingers into my wet,

warm core. "Patience, little bird. I will reward you." His hot breath fanned over my face, and I sighed against him, melting.

He ran his fingers from my core to my clit and back, soaking every inch with my wetness. My body rebelled with the need to explode around him. Nobody had touched me like this. He flicked my clit, and I arched up into his chest.

"Good girl, Harley. You're fucking soaked for me, little bird." I was light-headed from not breathing, but I nodded. East hummed his approval and pressed his thumb against my clit, while he worked the other two fingers inside of me.

I cried out, unable to stop myself from grinding on him. His slow strokes were driving me insane with need, and a shudder ran through me when he quickened his pace.

I whimpered, clutching at him with a desperation I'd never felt before. A long moan ripped from my chest as he added a third finger. *So full.*

He slowly circled my clit, stroking the heat inside me until I was drawn tight with tension that built every time I rocked my hips against his hand.

"Come, little bird. Sing for me, Harley." His low, raspy voice tipped me over the edge, and my head fell back as the pressure exploded through me, unlike anything I'd ever experienced before.

My core clenched greedily around his fingers, every part of me combusting. The release rocked me, and I screamed his name in the darkness of the room. His fingers slowly milked the rest of my orgasm as I watched the grin that tore at his lips.

"You're so fucking beautiful when you sing for me, little bird." He growled, and with one hand, he pushed the remaining boundary between us away. His boxers fell to the floor with a soft thud, his heavy length resting against my quivering heat.

His heart pounded against my chest as he closed the space between us. He stroked his length between my wet thighs, and I spread my legs, giving him access, drawing a deep groan from the back of his throat.

"I don't have a fucking condom," he growled, his body tensing.

"I'm on the pill," I whispered, absolutely breathless, my thighs quivering around his hips.

"Are you sure? Harley, we can stop. I can stop." His voice was so full of need, tearing at my soul.

"Don't stop. Please don't stop. I need you, Easton." He nodded and pressed the head of his cock to my slippery heat.

Lips parted, I pressed my forehead to his as he slowly worked himself between my folds, against my sensitive clit, and ground into me. My eyelids closed on their own accord, pleasure coursing through my body.

His movements were too gentle, caressing, like he was trying to savor this moment and my body. Too perfect for a moment that might never happen again. Perfect enough to ruin me for any other man.

He pressed soft kisses along my jaw. "Look at me, Harley. Open those beautiful eyes and look at me. I want you to see me and what I'm going to do to you."

Opening my eyes, his gaze pierced mine, his icy blue eyes clashing against mine, full of emotion neither of us was ready to express verbally. He nipped at my bottom lip, then caressed it with his tongue, hands sliding over my skin until every nerve ending screamed with need. He had set me on fire with his perfect words and touch.

I held his gaze as he pulled out and then entered me in one fluid thrust. A tortured moan escaped his lips as I screamed his name. The feeling of fullness overwhelmed every single one of my senses, and I squeezed around him with a need I'd never known before.

He was too controlled, body tight with restraint, his muscles tense beneath my touch. He kept up a steady pace, stroking me from the inside, and my heart clenched as he made love to me.

Suddenly, his hand skimmed over my sensitive skin until he found my clit. When he rubbed two fingers over it, I squirmed beneath him. I dropped my head onto the soft mattress, his name a broken plea on my lips.

I ground against him, needing more, but he remained slow and teasing. I was sure my body was breaking as he thrust his length into my core. Easton shook as he drove in and out of me, building the pressure we were both so desperate for.

"Open your eyes, Harley," he rasped, voice low. Looking at him, I focused on his mouth and the tiny bead of sweat on his top lip. Moving my gaze up toward his eyes, his hungry gaze ate me whole.

His fingers brushed against my clit harder, his hips picked up speed, and I was a second away from breaking.

"Come for me, Harley. Sing, my little bird. Sing for me," he growled, and I shattered, his name like a long-lost prayer on my lips.

He paused, buried deep inside me, and then he raised himself off me, his length gone, and then he thrust back into me with such force, I screamed as he groaned out my name, his hot seed filling me.

"Fuck, Harley. Fuck. Fuck." He dropped his head to my sweaty shoulder and blew out a deep breath. "You're fucking incredible, little bird."

He got up from the bed, disappearing into what I imagined was the bathroom. He emerged a beat later, and suddenly, there was a warm cloth at my entrance. I jumped in surprise.

"What are you doing?" I reached for him, but he put a hand on my shoulder, pushing me back down.

"Taking care of you, Harley. Treating you the way you deserve, baby." I sank back into the soft duvet, falling unconditionally in love with this man.

A minute later, he went back into the bathroom. Then, he was back just as quickly as he'd gone, his hands going underneath my heavy body, pulling me into his arms.

"What are you doing now?" I slurred, longing to just fall asleep.

"Putting you inside my bed." He threw the duvet back and then the top sheet before laying me back down. I sank into the silk sheets, my head landing on the softest pillow.

"This bed is magic," I whispered, curling into his body as he got in beside me. Dragging me up to his chest, he fell back onto the pillows and kissed me softly, cherishing my mouth.

Curled into him, I never wanted to move again. His arms were wrapped around me, his heartbeat under my ear. I listen to it slow, no longer the sound of hummingbird's wings. I pressed a kiss to his chest, and he stroked my arm, his fingers causing goosebumps to rise in their wake.

I nuzzled closer to him, my eyes drooping closed, and I fell asleep in a man's arms for the first time in my life.

Chapter Sixteen

EASTON

Sunlight streamed through the windows in my bedroom, I forgot to close the blinds last night, my mind in a haze with my desperation to have Harley. She was no longer draped over my chest, and instead, she was curled up on the other side of the bed, her dark hair fanned out over the pillow, soft snores coming from her parted lips.

I never thought I'd be here. Calling an apartment mine with a king-size bed with the perfect woman sleeping in it.

In one of Harley's letters, she mentioned more than once that she strongly believed everything happened for a reason.

Was that why we met?

Was that why I was set up all those years ago?

If I hadn't been arrested, would I have met her?

Shaking the thoughts from my head, I got up from the bed. Raising my arms above my head, I stretched out my back and reached for my toes. My muscles and bones creaked with the simple movement, my age showing. I pulled the curtain drapes closed, as not to wake her with the electric blinds. The room was once again bathed in shadow, ensuring her a little more sleep.

I had woken her up an hour after we fell asleep for another round, and she'd been eager to have me buried deep inside her again. My dick pulsed at the thought, and I glanced over at her. Her bare shoulder peaked out from the thin, silk sheet, making my mouth water.

I couldn't get enough of her.

"I can feel you looking at me," her voice was hoarse from screaming my name.

"You're supposed to sleep in." I edged closer to the bed, thinking about how I was going to make her sing for me.

"You left the bed." She turned over and opened her eyes, blinking slowly. She rubbed her one eye and then groaned. "Fuck." She jumped from the bed, running for the bathroom, and I followed close behind her.

"What's wrong, Harley?" She was standing on her toes, trying to look at her eye in the mirror. "Harley?"

"My contact. it's moved. I'm not supposed to sleep with it in. I forgot." Her voice shook with panic, and I gently gripped her elbow.

"Here. Let me look." She turned to me, Biting down on her bottom lip, she nervously nodded.

I found the thin, almost clear film instantly. Quickly washing my hands, I used one finger to hold her eyelid open and the other to pinch it out.

She immediately snapped her eyes shut and sighed in relief as I held the flimsy plastic on my finger, inspecting the blue contact.

Slowly opening her eyes, she turned from me, but I saw a flash of green. "Harley, don't you have two contacts?" I asked, dropping the contact to the counter and reaching for her.

"No, just one. I, uh, need to go." She brushed past me and bent down to pick up her discarded bra and thong from the night before.

I latched onto her bicep and turned her into my chest. Startled, she looked up at me, and I saw her first secret.

No longer was she looking up at me with two blue eyes, but rather one was blue and the other green. She sighed, her shoulders slumping in defeat.

"Now you know."

"Why were you hiding it from me?" I cradled her face with my hand, and she tensed.

"I hate being different." As she looked at me with two of the most beautiful eyes I'd ever seen, I struggled to find the right words to say without scaring her away.

"I like it. I really fucking like it."

"You do?" Her voice was weak, no longer the strong, confident woman from last night.

"Yeah, baby, I really do. Please don't hide from me. You and I," I placed my hand over her heart, where it thrummed wildly against my palm, "we don't keep secrets. We're on the same team."

She nodded, a small smile curving her lips. "There's a we?" She giggled at my eye roll.

"You doubted that after last night? I'm not a kid anymore, Harley. I'm not looking to play games or for one-night-stands. I want someone to share the rest of my life with. We've spent the last year learning about each other through letters, and now, I want to do the same in person." I kissed her nose, and her smile broadened.

"You know that means meeting my parents." She raised a brow, and I could almost read her mind—the very parents who were strangely never around.

"I'll do anything for you."

"Does breakfast count? I'm starving." Her stomach rumbled, confirming her statement.

"Let's shower and then whip something up together."

"Okay. I only need five minutes." She pulled out of my grasp, but I grabbed her hand and pulled her back to me.

"Together, Harley. You know, conserve water and all that crap." Her eyes went wide, and a beautiful blush crept up her neck and across her cheeks.

"You don't look like the conserving type?" she teased, but I was already scooping her into my arms and walking into the bathroom.

"I need you," I whispered, kissing her cheek.

"I need you more."

* * *

"So, you know how to cook," Harley pointed out, staring at me in wonder as I whipped us up some scrambled eggs and bacon.

Her hair was wet, dripping down the back of my shirt from last night, and I was itching to find a good enough reason why I shouldn't take it off her and devour her instead of the food.

"*Mm*, yes. My foster mother taught me and Gray." I flinched at the slip, but when I glanced at her over my shoulder, her eyes were wide with curiosity.

"Gray?" She focused again on the coffee she'd been making us.

"My foster brother," I answered, wishing to evade further questions, and she seemed to understand.

"My mom never taught me how to cook, and I don't have a kitchen in my dorm, so I haven't had a need to cook." She filled the silence easily, distracting me from thoughts of my past.

"I'll teach you."

"Really?" Her voice picked up an octave in excitement. The smallest things brought her such joy. I was learning more and more about her, despite a year of sharing letters and secrets.

"You're not what I pictured all this time." I dished up the eggs on two plates, and then the bacon, before setting it down on the placemats she found on the kitchen counter.

She was getting up on the barstool, her eyes watching me cautiously. "Let me guess, covered in tattoos and red hair?" She twirled a lock of her dark, wet hair around her finger with a small smile.

"No. I wasn't expecting you to be so short, for starters." She laughed, picking up her fork, she started eating the food I prepared.

"Well, I certainly wasn't going to mention my height in a

letter, East." I rolled my eyes at her quick wit, letting her claim another piece of my broken heart.

"You're kind," I continued with my description, and she blushed.

"You didn't get that from me joining the program, to begin with?"

"We both know you needed to do that to graduate, just like I needed it to get out. Speaking of, when do you graduate?" She had polished off her plate of food and was jumping down from the barstool, giving me her back in response. "Harley?" I questioned, following her into the kitchen where she started the dishes.

"This week."

"And the problem with that?" I pressed, putting my plate in the dishwasher. Wrapping my hands around her small wrists, I forced her to stop and look at me. She tried to cover her face with her hair, but I saw through the thin wisps.

Unshed tears shone in her beautiful blue and green eyes.

"My parents won't be able to make it." Her parents continued to surprise me. How could they have raised her to be so kind when they were so cruel?

"Did they say why?" She nodded, and I let go of one of her wrists to brush away her wet hair.

"It's not a big enough reason for them to come see me." Anger flooded my body at her shrug at their disgusting behavior. "But that's okay. I don't want to see them anyway."

She blinked slowly, swallowed thickly, and then plastered a fake smile to her swollen lips. Always putting on a brave face.

I wanted to get past her armor. I needed her to know it was okay to tell me the truth. I needed to be her safe space.

"You don't have to put on a smile for me, little bird." I softly brushed my thumb along her plump, swollen, bottom lip.

"It's better this way," she insisted, her lips moving against my finger.

"For you or me?" I whispered, fighting every urge in my body to press my lips to hers.

"Everyone. I won't beg them to be there, and I won't make my problems yours or anyone else's." She pulled away from me again, but I tightened my hold on her wrist and dropped my other hand to her waist.

"Don't pull away from me, Harley. Let me in." She tugged her wrist from my hold and then took a quick step back.

"We barely know each other. Why would I suddenly let you in?" I tried to reign in the hurt. Swallowing thickly, I saw the storm brewing in her eyes. Her bottom lips quivered, and her chest rose and fell quickly.

"What else do you want to know about me, Harley? I spent the last year answering every question you asked me. I put all my secrets down for you on paper. What else do you need from me?" She took another step back, bumping into the kitchen counter.

I could easily close the distance between us. Two steps and I would be caging her in, giving her no chance of escape, but I didn't move.

"I need to know you'll still be here now that I got you out of prison. I need to know that you aren't going to leave me, too." Her voice shook, and I took a step closer to her, but she wrapped her arms around her torso, making me pause.

"I'm not leaving. You weren't just a get-out-of-jail card, Harley. This isn't fucking Monopoly." I gritted out the words, and her gaze fell to the ground.

"You still haven't told me what got you in prison in the first place, East. You haven't shared all your secrets. Just like I didn't share all of mine. Who knows how many more still exist between us?" I balled my hands into fists, hating her truth.

"You want to know why I served five years? You need me to tell you how I was betrayed by my foster brother? Do you want the details of how my foster father abused me and Gray for years? Do you really need to see all my broken pieces to let me give you the rest of what I have left? Tell me, Harley. What do you need?"

A soft cry escaped her trembling lips, and I hated myself for causing her more pain, but she'd turned what I had hoped to be a good fucking morning into a shitshow. She wasn't the fucking victim here.

"I don't know what I'm doing here," she whispered, turning away from me, her body shaking with silent tears.

"What do you mean?" My voice was low. I failed to keep my own pain from lacing the question.

She turned and charged at me, jabbing her finger against my chest. "I don't even know you, and I just had sex with you. I'm standing here in your kitchen fighting with you for no fucking reason. You don't know me, Easton, and I don't fucking know who you are either."

Grabbing her hand, I interlocked our fingers. "You're wrong, Harley." Touching her heart, the familiar beat of a hummingbird's wings greeted me. I brought her hand to my heart, hoping she could feel the same. "Your heart knows me, little bird. And we're fighting because this matters. You fucking matter to me, Harley. I've had to fight my whole life for everything I have, and I will fucking fight for you, too."

"Stop doing this to me," she cried, dropping her head to my chest. "Stop being nice to me. I don't deserve it."

"Wrong again, little bird. I might not know every little secret about you, but I do know that you have a big heart. I know that it's been broken too many times, and I know that I will mend it. I also know that I will learn all your secrets because with time, you will let me in, just as I will with you. I know that your soul sings for mine, and you know how I know that?"

She shook her head, biting down on her fucking lip, which I wanted to bite with my own teeth. I pulled her lip from her teeth, running my thumb over it again, and she sighed.

"Because mine sings for you." Tears rolled down her already damp cheeks.

"I don't want to be hurt again," she whispered, sniffling.

"I can't make that promise. Don't make me. But I can

promise to do my best every day for you. I can promise to be faithful, to give you my heart, but I can't promise that you won't get hurt along the way."

"Everyone is going to think I'm crazy for falling for you."

"Who gives a fuck what everyone thinks?" I wiped away her hot tears and caressed her warm, wet cheeks.

"I do."

"If I make you happy, does it matter what they think?" She shook her head, and I sighed in relief.

"I want to take this slow," she whispered, and I groaned, throwing my head back.

"Too late for that, Harley. I know what you taste like. I'm addicted, and you're my drug. Move in with me." I dipped my head, brushing my nose against hers, my lips a breath away from hers.

"Slow, Easton."

"I don't want to go slow with you. I want to spend the rest of my life getting to know you." She giggled and pressed her lips against mine in a soft kiss. "Don't make me beg, my little bird."

"Perhaps I could be convinced," she teased, and I dropped my hands to her legs, picking her up. She wrapped her legs around my waist, her arms going around my neck.

"For starters, I live here," I whispered against her lips. "It's free. I have a big bed. Have you seen the kitchen? And did I mention I live here?" I teasingly repeated. She threw her head back with laughter, and I knew I'd won.

Fuck what everyone else thought. We were made for each other.

Chapter Seventeen

HARLEY

I HAD PASSED CRAZY AND WAS NOW DANGLING ON THE edge of insanity as I drove away from Easton's very luxurious apartment building back to the dorms with the Sunday evening sun setting in my rearview mirror.

I had one week left of class before graduation, and he had his first week at his new job. We agreed to take one week apart to give ourselves time to think about what was the best decision for us. Well, I did anyway, and he continued to suggest moving in with him right away, but I wasn't ready just yet.

I kept wondering what Kennedy would say and how my parents would react. If they would even care at all since they couldn't even find the time to come to my college graduation.

Easton was patient and kind as he listened to my fears and objections, and I tried to listen to him.

"Fuck them. Fuck anyone who judges us."

He said it over and over, and I wanted to believe his words. I wanted them to be my mantra, but fear plagued my mind, their judgmental voices screaming in my head.

What are you doing with him?

You're sleeping with an inmate?

You should be with someone better.

He's tainted.

He'll never give you the future you deserve.

We taught you better.

He has a criminal record.

You let his dirty hands touch you?

Shaking the evil from my mind, I tightened my grip on the leather steering wheel and tried to enjoy the late, summer sunset.

Every time I blinked, I saw Easton's gorgeous, soul-sucking eyes. Their clear, hypnotizing blue drawing me in, hook, line, and sinker.

His smile, perfectly white teeth that shined in the darkness of his bedroom, our skin glowing under the moonlight that streamed through his windows.

His burning touch, setting my skin aflame, my soul rising to meet his with every gentle stroke of his fingers or brush of his soft, full lips.

Heat crept up my neck, fanning across my cheeks at the memory of him. I gripped the steering wheel tighter, clenching my thighs at the heat coiling in my stomach. Goosebumps blazed a trail across my skin, and I squirmed in my seat.

Was our connection purely sexual? Or was it more?

I thought back to the way he held me this afternoon in his bed after making love to me. How he wrapped his big arms around me and listened to me talk about my parents. His strength never wavered, only surrounding me. *"You deserve better, my sweet little bird,"* he'd whispered in my ear, his lips kissing anything they could touch, soothing an ache so deep in my soul, I wept until I fell asleep.

Parking in the student lot at my dorm, I entered the quiet building. Everyone was either out for dinner or preparing for the next day. I stuck my key in the lock of my room and prayed Kennedy was out with her boyfriend tonight.

Stepping into our shared space, I checked her bed first, and lying there, hair a mess, makeup smudged under her eyes, tears rolling down her cheeks, sat my roommate.

"Kennedy, what's wrong?" I shut the door behind me, surveying the mess surrounding her. She had wrapped herself in a big blanket, her small body hidden beneath baggy pajamas, so unlike the girl I'd come to know.

"Aaron cheated on me!" she wailed. Grabbing a tissue from the box next to her, she blew obnoxiously loud into the paper. "He actually kissed another girl," she cried, continuing to blow her nose.

"I'm sorry. I'm so sorry." I crossed the small room and settled on the edge of her bed, wrapping my arms around her and offering my strength.

"I just can't believe he's embarrassed me like this. I have to show my face tomorrow on campus," she cried into my shoulder, her tears wetting my skin.

"It'll be okay. You have me," I tried to comfort her, but she shook her head.

"My face is going to be so swollen. My eyes. Oh, God, they are going to look terrible!"

Trust this girl to be crying over her appearance tomorrow.

"Then stop crying and do one of those face masks," I suggested, and she pulled away from me.

"You're a genius, Harley! Why didn't I think of that?" She jumped from the bed, running into the bathroom. I heard the water running from the sink faucet. "Oh, God, my face!" she shrieked, and I cringed.

Flopping back onto her bed, I closed my eyes while I waited for her.

"Okay, spill all the beans. You're glowing, which means you've just had the best sex of your life." She jumped onto the bed, making me bounce up, and I groaned, looking up at her. She was wearing a ridiculous face mask, her hair neatly pulled back into a perfect ponytail.

"It was the best sex of my life." She laughed and slapped my leg.

"Tell me all about him. Is it the guy you've been writing all those letters to?" I sat up, looking at her in shock, and she grinned sheepishly. "You didn't think I noticed, huh? I might have snooped on a few of them." She blushed, averting her gaze. "He sounds like a catch."

"You read my letters?" My jaw dropped at her little nod. "How long have you known?"

"About six months. Please don't be mad." She reached for my hand and squeezed it with both of hers. I struggled to hold in my laugh at her strange appearance but manage to mask my expression for her sake.

"I'm not. Just shocked. How much do you know?"

"Are you implying that he's an inmate?" I nodded, and she sighed, rolling her eyes. "Does he make you happy, Harley?" I nodded again, and she smiled.

"Then, it doesn't matter who he is or where he came from. Life is too short to be unhappy with anyone." Her eyes welled with tears. "I should have known better with Aaron. He's been making up a whole lot of excuses on why he couldn't see me recently."

As far as I knew, she was still seeing him the normal amount, although I hadn't seen him in our room for months.

"Where have you been going then?" I asked, holding her hands, sympathizing with her.

She choked on a sob. "The library or the mall. I didn't want anyone to find out."

"Oh, Kennedy, it's going to be okay." Pulling her into another hug, she sobbed in my arms, and I let her, a small connection between us forming with every minute that passed.

"When can I meet him?" She sniffled on my shoulder, and I cringed at the thought of whatever wet substance rolled down.

"He's coming to graduation, actually." She sat up and got off the bed, pulling the face mask off and washing her face.

"Do I look any better?" Her face was red and blotchy, but I lied and nodded, earning a sigh of relief from her. Surely, she would look better after a good night of sleep.

"I'm actually moving in with him after graduation." She dropped her phone that she had just picked up off the bed, and it bounced on the carpet by her feet.

"You're doing what?" she squealed, and I shrunk back. "That's amazing, Harley! I am so happy for you!" Her reaction was unexpected but welcomed, so when she threw her arms around me, I hugged her back.

An hour later, we had shared the events of our weekend, and we were both lying in our own beds in the darkness.

"Hey, Kennedy?"

"Yeah, Har?"

"Why couldn't this have happened sooner?" I didn't elaborate, scared to put a name on our sort-of friendship.

"I guess because everything happens for a reason, right? At least, I like to believe that." She said exactly what I had been thinking, and my heart soared at my favorite mantra.

"I wish we could have been friends sooner."

"Me, too, but I'm glad it happened this way."

* * *

THE WEEK FLEW BY, and before I knew it, I was standing outside Easton's apartment door, two hours before graduation. The lobby man had to call to let me up the elevator, so I knew he was expecting me, but I was suddenly afraid to knock on the big door.

What if a week apart had given him time to think?

Just as I raised my fist to knock, the door flew open, and East's scent engulfed me as did his arms. He dragged me into the apartment, the door swinging shut behind him. His lips found mine, and every fear evaporated just as quickly as I thought them.

78

"I thought you weren't coming," he whispered against my lips, his minty breath fanning my face.

"As if I could possibly stay away." I pressed my lips to his, our tongues fighting for dominance. But in the end, I let him win, and he walked me back until my back hit the door. He caged me in.

"How much time do we have?" he rasped, desire lacing every word.

"None. Kennedy is waiting downstairs to meet you." He pulled back, raising a brow.

"Your roommate, Kennedy?" I nodded, and he took a step back. I got my first real look at him, noticing his new shoes, freshly-ironed slacks, and a white button-up shirt tucked perfectly into his navy pants.

"New clothes?" He rolled his eyes and shrugged.

"I've got a lot to tell you."

"Good or bad?" I waited for him to grab whatever he needed from the kitchen, and he surprised me with a fresh bouquet of daisies.

"For you, grad!" He pressed a soft kiss to my cheek and then opened the front door, ushering me out. "Good and bad, I guess. I'm not really sure. Depends how you want to look at it. But we can talk about it later tonight. This afternoon is all about you, Harley." Linking my fingers through his, I let him lead me downstairs to my running car in the parking lot.

"We've become friends," I informed him just as the passenger door on my car opened, and Kennedy burst out, her hand outstretched toward East.

"Good Lord, you are good-looking. Do you have any friends?" Kennedy blushed, and I cringed, but Easton chuckled.

"None good enough for you. Nice to meet you, Kennedy."

"Darn. My boyfriend just dumped me, and I was hoping to bring a total hottie to the party tonight." She slid into the backseat of my car, and East held open the passenger door for me.

Kennedy slapped my shoulder as he rounded the front of my

car, and I turned to her, catching a wink and cheesy grin. "Wow!" she whispered as he got in the car and shifted it into drive.

"Directions?" I showed him the route on my phone, and we fell into an easy conversation on the short drive.

"What are your plans for after college?" Easton asked Kennedy, looking at her in the rearview mirror. Our hands were linked on my center console, his thumb rubbing the top of my hand soothingly.

"Going back home to my parents, actually. They're supposed to have some friend hiring at the local florist, which will give me time to figure out what I actually want to do because I am lost." East chuckled, and Kennedy nervously giggled. "Sounds familiar, right?"

"I think every grad has the same idea. No harm in that. As long as you don't get comfortable with that job and find your true purpose, I don't see anything wrong." I listened, wondering about my own future.

I hadn't secured a job yet, and besides, all the local journalist positions were full at the moment.

"What do you do for a living?" Kennedy asked, and for the first time, I realized I didn't even know what Easton's been doing for the last week.

He coughed, his hand becoming tense in mine. "Construction."

"Oh, so you're really good with your hands." She giggled, and I blushed, remembering just how good he was.

An hour later, Kennedy and I were sitting in our designated seats, but my gaze remained on Easton, who was grinning at me like I was some rare gem. My heart somersaulted at the way he watched me. When my name was called, he screamed, and Kennedy joined him. I nearly tripped going up the three steps on the stage, but when I looked out into the sea of people, I saw Easton standing, clapping his hands. And I knew deep down in my heart...

He was a good man.

The rest of the ceremony passed quickly, and before I knew it, we were saying goodbye to Kennedy and getting back into my car, heading to his apartment for the night. We'd eaten celebratory cake with Kennedy, and the urge to expel it from my body was bubbling in my chest.

I'd barely eaten the entire week to fit in my dress for tonight. And whatever I did eat came right back up. I wanted to be thin. I needed to have the perfect body for him.

As soon as we entered his apartment, I rushed for the bathroom, throwing the seat up. I retched into the toilet until everything I ate in the last hour came up. Quickly brushing my teeth, I wiped my mouth, fixed my hair, and unlocked the bathroom door.

Checking my appearance one last time, I didn't see Easton standing right there until I slammed right into his broad chest.

"Are you sick, Harley?" Worry plagued his tone, and I stepped back.

"No, of course not. I just needed the bathroom real quick." I reached for his hand, but he shook his head, stopping me.

"I heard you."

"It isn't what you're thinking," I defended, but his mouth settled into a frown.

"And what exactly am I thinking, Harley?"

"I'm not pregnant."

"Didn't think you were."

Fear settled in my gut, and my hands grew clammy. "I must have eaten something bad earlier, that's all," I assured him, trying again to close the distance between us, but he shook his head yet again.

"Don't try and play me the fool, Harley. I saw you last weekend and again today. You're malnourished. I know what you're doing." Disappointment flashed in his eyes, and this time, I took a step back.

No. He doesn't know. He can't know. No one can.

I shook my head. I watched his lips move. I heard his words, but I refused to accept it. He didn't know me. He didn't understand. No one understood.

If I could be perfect, have the perfect body, then he wouldn't leave. He wouldn't be like my parents. I wouldn't disappoint him.

But the two words that left his mouth brought me to my knees as they echoed in the small bathroom.

Eating disorder.

Chapter Eighteen

EASTON

ONE WEEK AGO

The Monday morning rays of sunlight beat down heavily on my head, and humidity weighed down my every step, but I push through, following the directions Rick printed out for me few days ago. Today was my first day of work, and I didn't want to be late. Hopefully, I could find the owner of this company and find out why he was offering a recent inmate so much.

I hadn't even been given a name, just an address and time to be there. Glancing down at the crumbled paper in my hand and then back up at the glass building in front of me, I confirmed the address and reached for the door.

Andy's Construction

The silver sign stood tall and proud on the front of the building, almost blinding me.

Stepping into the air-conditioned building, my shoes squeaked against the clean tiles, and my gaze instantly shot to an elderly lady working the lobby desk. She was busy stapling papers together, her attention occupied.

Walking up to the desk, I waited for her to finish before clearing my throat, startling her despite my efforts not to.

"Oh, heavens. I'm sorry, dear. I didn't see you come in." She placed a hand on her chest, and guilt surged through me.

"My apologies, ma'am. I'm wondering if you could help me. I'm supposed to be starting today. My name is—" she interrupts me, placing her wrinkled hand on one of mine that rested on the glass edge of the desk.

"You're Easton Diggs. You look just like him," she said, taking her hand away and dialing a number on her desk phone.

It rang twice before a man's voice echoed in the lobby. "Andy speaking. How may I help you?"

"He's here," she said and then put the phone down, not waiting for a response. Eyeing her, she seemed to sense my unease and curved her cherry-red lips into a soft smile. "You've been a huge topic of conversation around here, Easton. We've been eagerly awaiting this day."

I wanted to question the hidden meaning of her words. I needed to understand the emotion in her blue eyes.

Why was she looking at me like that? Was she afraid of me? Did everyone know I was a convict? Did they know I had no choice? Would I be treated differently here?

"Straight to the elevator, son. Go up to the tenth floor." She pointed to two silver elevators behind her, and I followed her directions, muscles tensing as I pressed the silver up arrow and waited.

The elevator doors flew open with a loud beep that echoed off the walls, startling me. Trying to shake off the nerves, I stepped inside and released a deep breath, relaxing my tense shoulders. I pressed the tenth-floor button and let the elevator take me to the highest floor in the building.

The numbers ticked by slowly, and sweat gathered at the nape of my neck. My heartbeat increased with every number, and I struggled to calm my erratic breathing.

Be calm, Easton. Harley believes in you.

The elevator doors opened, and I stepped onto the tenth floor. My sneaker squeaked on the clean floor as I took in the gray desk across from me. A man and woman were sitting there, their heads bent together as they whispered behind a big computer screen. The room was surrounded by floor-to-ceiling glass windows that illuminated the room with blinding clarity.

The air was crisp with the scent of lavender, and I inhaled a shaky breath. My shirt was suddenly too tight, the collar pressing uncomfortably against my throat as I swallowed past the lump. I cleared my throat, preparing to announce my arrival, but they both stood and rounded the desk.

They want you here.

"Good morning," My voice cracked with nerves, and I shut my mouth, my steps halting as they continue to close the distance between us.

The woman was teetering on a pair of black heels, similar to the ones Harley was wearing Saturday night, but her steps were full of purpose, unlike Harley, who took each step with each calculated deliberation. She was dressed in a pair of black pants and a tight-fitting, white button-down shirt, her black hair pulled back into a slick ponytail that swished with every step.

Her red lips curved into a too-big smile, showcasing perfect, straight white teeth. There was a dimple tugging at the corner of both her lips, but what captured my attention were her ice-blue eyes.

Beside her was a tall man. His dark hair was in disarray, frown lines marring his forehead, and his brows furrowed. His dark eyes were focused on me, their gaze intense, searching. A light dusting of gray hair shadowed his jawline, and his lips remained turned down. He was dressed similarly to the woman in a white button-down shirt and black pants, shiny leather shoes clipping against the wood floor.

They stopped a mere five feet away from me, and I waited, watching them look me over. *What were they expecting? Do they like what they see? Do I look like a criminal?*

"We've been waiting a long time to meet you, Easton." The

woman's voice was *welcoming*, soft and feminine, and the scent of her floral perfume tickled my nose.

"Thank you for this opportunity. I really appreciate you taking a chance on me." I stepped closer to them, extending my hand to her. She paused, her eyes assessing as they glanced between my outreached hand and my face.

She closed the space, throwing her arms around me instead, her soft cries echoing around us as she wept into my neck. My eyes widened in surprise, and I stiffened.

"Layla," the man growled, and I stiffened further beneath her. She didn't loosen her hold, instead tightening it. "You promised," he whispered.

"He's here, Andy. He's real."

I looked at the man standing behind her, and the sadness and relief in his gaze was staggering. He cleared his throat, opened his mouth, but said nothing.

The woman released me and stepped back, wiping at her misty eyes. "Oh, God, I wasn't supposed to do that." She laughed nervously through her tears. I wanted to understand the silent conversation they shared with one look, but the voice in my head had me stepping away from them.

"I don't understand." I looked between them, searching for an answer to their weird behavior but received none.

"We weren't going to tell you like this. I wasn't supposed to," Layla started to explain but then choked on her emotion.

Andy stepped closer, and putting his hand on her shoulder, he finished for her, "We're your parents, Easton."

"No." I stepped back again, my back hitting the closed elevator doors. The cold seeped through the thin material of my shirt, shocking me, but I couldn't move. "I don't have parents."

Layla clutched her chest with a loud sob. Andy wrapped his arms around her, holding her up as her knees buckled beneath her weight.

"It's true. I'm sorry. I'm so sorry," she cried, her wails of desperation echoing around us. "I thought I made the right choice. I thought I did. I'm sorry."

Andy's dark eyes were drowning in unspoken emotion as he held up whom I presumed to be his wife. She fell apart, her sobs getting louder with each passing moment. I hated seeing women cry. Because I hated hearing my foster mother cry when our foster father beat her. I hated the weakness I associated with it.

"I don't have parents." I swallowed thickly, wishing I hadn't come here today. I didn't need this. I didn't want their charity. I didn't need this job; I would find another. I didn't need more abusers in my life.

Giving them my back, I pressed the elevator button repeatedly, needing to get fresh air. The walls were closing in, and I couldn't think straight with her cries bouncing around us.

"Please don't go." Andy's gruff voice was soft, broken.

The doors opened, and I hesitated when her cries increased. "Andy, please. Andy! He's leaving!" Her voice pierced my heart, and I turned to look at Layla fighting her husband, trying to get to me.

The elevator doors closed, and my opportunity to flee was gone.

Analyzing their appearances, I noted the similarities between me and them. I saw my eyes in hers, and my facial structure mirrored Andy's. They could be telling the truth, or they could be lying. Just like my foster father lied about finding my real parents. Just like Gray lied that night.

I couldn't trust them. I owed it to myself to leave, but I couldn't move my fucking feet, not with Layla's ice-blue eyes piercing me, begging me to stay.

"Show him, Andy. Show him." Andy released her, and with quick strides to his big desk, he started throwing papers around until he found whatever he was looking for. Layla held herself, her chest heaving with soft sobs, her eyes scanning me.

Andy walked past his wife and thrust an old, wrinkled paper into my hands. My eyes skimmed over the big, bold letters.

Certificate of Birth
Child's Name: Easton Ryder Briggs
Date of Birth: April 12th

"This doesn't prove anything." I didn't look up as I continued to scan the contents of the certificate. Once I had finished going through the document, I looked up at the two strangers I was starting to believe might just be my parents.

"We were sixteen when I fell pregnant with you. Seventeen when you were born and in no way prepared to take care of a child. Your father and I grew up in a trailer park on the edge of town, with nothing to our names and parents who didn't want anything to do with a baby." Layla, my mother, wiped her wet cheeks and stepped away from Andy to close the space between us.

"It's been twenty-six fucking years," I gritted, seeing the resemblance in their faces more and more and wishing it wasn't there.

"We've been trying to find you. When we found the adoption agency, they'd changed your last name to protect you from my parents," Layla said, and I waited for her to explain why I would need protection from people who didn't want me.

"Layla's father, Bill, was an evil man who used children to do his bidding around town." *It couldn't be.* "We wanted to give you a better life, one we couldn't provide at the time. You have to understand, Easton, we've been looking for you for years. The adoption agency you came from burned down a year after you were adopted and lost all their paperwork. There was no trace of you ever existing besides that." Andy nodded toward the birth certificate in my trembling hands.

"Bill Cutco adopted me, and my foster brother, Gray Hughes." I struggled to avoid crumpling the stupid fucking paper in my hands, the only thing linking me to these people in front of me.

"No," Layla gasped, her hand wrapping around my forearm, her touch soft and gentle, everything I imagined it would be.

"Guess your father did find me. Sacrificing me and then

taking away the life I should have had with two parents didn't save me from him. He still fucking found me." Rage slithered through my veins, tensing my muscles. I fought the familiar ache in my chest, and my scars burned almost as if they were fresh at the reminder of that man.

"Why didn't you find him, Andy?! I begged you to find him." Layla's hand tightened around my arm, but her touch did nothing to soothe the hatred. Instead, it intensified.

"I hired every goddamn PI in town to find him; you know that, Layla. I did every fucking thing I could besides knocking on your father's door," Andy growled at her. Anger rippled through the air, and I fed off it. I ripped my arm from her touch. I didn't want to feel her empathy now.

I needed my parents years ago.

I didn't need these people now.

"I have to go. You can take everything back—the job, the apartment. I don't need anything from you. I've survived without you for twenty-six years. I don't need your handouts."

"No, please, no! Don't go. Give me—us—a chance." My mother had latched onto me again, her nails biting into my skin.

"Let go of me! I don't fucking owe you a thing." Yanking my arm from her again, I turned away from her and Andy and pressed the elevator button repeatedly.

"Easton, son. Please." Andy's deep voice penetrated my walls, the one fucking word I'd yearned to be called my whole life, jilting my foundation.

"I am not your son," I seethed, seeing dark spots invade my vision as rage clouded all my logic.

"Whether you want to admit it or not, you are our fucking son. You have your mother's eyes and hair, and my goddamn nose and stubborn pride. We aren't asking you to forgive us. We are asking for a chance to get to know you and the man you've become. And until you are ready, the apartment is yours, the car in the parking garage is yours, and the job is yours. We made mistakes, Easton, like all teenagers do, and we are trying to do what is best for you."

Whirling around, I watched Andy pull his wife into his arms. She cried into his chest, and my heart splintered.

Did Bill beat her, too?

Did she know what her father was capable of?

Did she know what he made me do?

Did they know I was broken?

"You don't know what is best for me because you don't fucking know me," I gritted through clenched teeth.

"Then give us a chance to get to know you, Easton. Let us be there for you however you need." I didn't want to see the similarities, but I couldn't fight that he was right. I couldn't argue that I didn't have my mother's eyes and hair.

I couldn't fight because it was true.

The people I had been waiting to save me were finally here. But it was too fucking late to be saved.

"I don't want special treatment. I just need a job, and I will pay you back for the apartment and everything else."

Layla shook her head and opened her mouth to argue, but Andy stopped her.

"You don't want special treatment, boy? You want to mop the fucking floors? Do you want us to treat you like a recent inmate, is that it? Will it stroke your fucking ego to be treated like dirt?"

His words were worse than any beating I'd received in the last five years.

I didn't want to be just an inmate. I wanted to be Easton Diggs, the boy who had dreams before going to jail.

"Whatever helps you sleep at night." I swallowed the rage burning inside my chest.

"Stop this! I won't be part of any of this cruelty. I hurt you; we hurt you. My father hurt you. And I won't ever be able to apologize or grovel enough to show you just how much I regret my choices. But Easton, I can spend the rest my life showing you how much I love you and want you in my life." Layla, my mother, then turned and slapped Andy in the chest and pushed him away, inching closer to me, her steps slow and calculated.

"You'll never be able to erase it," I whispered, seeing the understanding and pain flickering in her eyes. She endured his abuse, too. She knew everything.

"Nobody will," she whispered, closing the space and wrapping me in her small arms, her strength surrounding me with the simple gesture. "But it doesn't mean I don't understand it, Easton. I know what a monster he was, and I'm sorry I couldn't protect you from him, but I will help you heal. Your father and I will help you. You just have to let us in."

"I was framed." I choked on my truth, fighting to reign in my trembling emotions. "I was going to leave him, and instead, he turned on me."

"I know, baby; I know. I'm sorry. I'm so sorry. My poor boy, you've had the world on your shoulders. You aren't alone anymore. You'll never be alone again." She held me to her small frame, and despite my best efforts, I broke, my walls collapsing with her touch and voice.

Chapter Nineteen

HARLEY

Easton's sharp blue eyes cut through me like glass. Disappointment swam in their icy depths, and I shriveled up under his hard glare.

"Don't worry about me," I whispered, standing to slam the door in his face, but he stopped me. Sticking out his hand, the force of his strength sent me to the ground in shock.

"Don't hide from me, Harley. We don't keep secrets," he reminded me, our argument from last weekend coming to the front of my mind. I couldn't believe we were having another one so soon.

If we had stuck to writing letters, we wouldn't be in this mess. He wouldn't know my biggest secret.

"We don't keep secrets? Then why the fuck were you arrested, East?" The words tasted like acid on my tongue, and the hurt that rippled across his face was far worse than any of the thoughts that plagued my mind.

"You want to take out your anger on me? You think I'm clipping your wings by making you face the fucking truth? I want you to fly, Harley. Don't you ever forget that. I'll trap you inside of a cage until I make you see your worth, little bird. And when you realize how powerful and beautiful you are, I'll show you how to fly again. And only then will you truly soar, my little bird."

I teared up at his words, at the tone of his voice, at the love shining in his eyes, and hated myself a little more for the person I had become.

"Tell me, East. Why must I share all my secrets when you've hidden the biggest one? We've been beating around the bush for a year now, and you still won't tell me. What are you so afraid of?" I screamed, standing up to face him.

The fucker had the audacity to grin, the most devastatingly handsome smile, that made my knees knock together with my love for him.

"Losing you." He swallowed and I took a step back.

"You can't mean that," I whispered, some of the anger deflating with his vulnerability. I didn't know I meant so much to him. He'd never voiced his feelings like that, gone that raw, and I sure as hell couldn't read his mind.

"You are the only person I care about, Harley. I don't need anyone or anything else as long as I have you by my side." Shaking my head, I pushed past him, and my hands sank through the material of his crisp white button-up, the curve of his hard abs just beneath my fingertips nearly drew a moan from my lips.

"Where the hell are you going?" Easton followed me through his apartment. I grabbed my bag from the kitchen counter and shoved my feet into my heels from earlier. My feet ached as I slipped the thin strap around my ankle.

My fingers grasped the bronze handle of his front door. Throwing the door open, I stepped into the carpeted hallway.

I had to get out.

I had to get away from *him*.

I needed air.

"Harley, don't run away from me!" His calloused fingers wrapped around my bicep, tugging me back into the apartment.

"Let me go. You have to let me go. I can't do this. I can't." The walls were closing in, and I sucked in a sharp breath, my lungs burning with the lack of oxygen, black dots swimming in my vision.

"I'm never letting you go, little bird. Don't make me do the impossible." I fell to my knees, and he was there, holding me, his touch setting my skin ablaze. His lips ghosted over my cheek, soft, warm, and soothing.

"You weren't supposed to find out!" I cried, curling into a ball, holding my shaky legs together with my weak arms. He wrapped himself around me, holding me together as I fell apart.

"I don't care. I just want you, my perfect little bird."

Chocking on a sob, I shook my head. *Perfect.* I was so far from it.

"There's nothing perfect about me," I cried, my chest heaving with sobs. His arms only tightened their possessive hold.

"I was framed for dealing drugs at a club by my foster brother," he whispered near my ear, and a new pain sliced at my broken heart—pain for him. "Gray changed our plan at the last minute to get home to his pregnant girlfriend faster, and I fell hook, line, and sinker because I trusted him. I vowed never to trust anyone again after that day."

Taking a slow deep breath, I slowed my racing heart and listened to his confession.

"Then, you wrote me a fucking letter, and that all went to hell because I can't deny you anything. My biggest secret is of being betrayed by the man I called my brother, not because I want to hide it from you, but because I am ashamed." He pulled away from me, the security of his touch no longer wrapped around me.

I looked at him through blurry eyes. Waiting for him to yell, like my parents had, like my school therapist had, like everyone had.

Instead, he cradled my face in his big hands, his fingers sinking into my hair, thumbs swiping at the hot tears rolling down my cheeks.

This man always surprised me.

"I don't want you to be ashamed. I don't want you to hide. I want you to live, Harley. I want you to eat whatever the fuck you want. I need you to love your body because if you don't, I'm going to lose you. I thought prison was my hell, but a life without you in it is not worth living. I need you to learn to love this beautiful body."

He pressed the softest kiss to my cheek, and the noise that tore from my throat was raw and broken. "Please don't cry, little bird. Please, baby, I can't fucking breathe when you cry."

I wanted to stop. I hated being so weak, but his words were my undoing. He was my biggest weakness. I wanted to be *perfect* for him.

"Your eyes bring me peace." He leaned forward and kissed my eyelids before leaning back, his artic eyes roaming over my body.

"What are you doing, East?" I whispered.

"Showing you everything I love about your body." I hiccupped on a cry, butterflies erupting from their dormant cocoons in my stomach and wreaking havoc.

Picking up my hands, he kissed each fingertip. "These fingers shared the secrets of your heart long before I knew it was meant to be mine. They made me fall in love with you with each perfectly written word."

Kissing a trail of heat up my one forearm to my shoulder, he did the same to the other, a wicked grin tugging at his ruggedly, beautiful face. "Arms that wrap around me while I'm making love to you, pulling our bodies impossibly closer together."

"You don't have to do this," I whispered as he lowered himself to my flat stomach and pressed a soft kiss through the thin material of my dress. I moaned.

"A perfect stomach to one day grow our babies." Heat crawled up my neck and into my cheeks at his comment, but he didn't deter from his mission.

He picked up my one foot and gently took off the heel, then repeated the same to the other. Massaging the soles of my feet, he grinned. "Beautiful toes that curl with each orgasm I give you. Two perfect feet that brought you to The Rose to meet me."

"Easton, really, I get it." I squirmed uncomfortably, but he shook his head.

"I am not done, Harley." He kissed a trail up my calves, and goosebumps skated up my spine. Heat pooled in my belly at the simple action. "Gorgeous legs made to wrap around my waist when I'm deep inside of you."

His lips moved against the soft skin of my thigh, and his head peaked under my short dress. I sighed in relief when his lips skimmed over my quivering heat. "I don't think I need to remind you of this beautiful pussy that weeps for me, how it sucks the cum from my cock. Do I, Harley?" he teased, his hot breath blowing against my hot center.

"Remind me, East," I whimper.

"You need me to remind you how perfect your pussy is, Harley?" he growled, and I unashamedly pushed my heat into his mouth, wishing I had listened to Kennedy and skipped underwear tonight.

His lips were perfectly soft and just a tease of what I could have before he pulled away. His eyes were bright with desire for me. Crawling over me, he stopped just in front of my face and kissed my lips like I was made of porcelain.

"Most importantly, my perfect little bird, you have these fucking lips. They bring me to my knees with the smallest smile and suck my soul right out of my body with one kiss. I don't care what you look like; I don't care if you are thin, fat, or in between. All I care is that you are here with me, that every night your warm body is curled around mine. I can't lose you to this disease. I won't survive." He gripped my chin and forced our eyes to lock, his brows furrowed in determination. "Do you understand me?"

I want to tell him I understood, but I'd be lying. I didn't understand how his love for a body I hated was infinite. What happened when I put on the extra weight? Would he love me then? Would he have still brought me home that night?

"You're thinking too much. Don't you understand, Harley? I'm not in love with your body." He pauses, and my heart stilled with his words. "I'm in love with your soul, baby. Your body is just a vessel. We won't take it with us when we leave."

"I hate my body," I cried, finally saying my truth out loud for the first time.

"Let me teach you how to love it, Harley. Don't run from me, from the future we are going to have. Please, little bird, let me teach you how to fly." We were still on the floor of his entrance, my back pressed into the floor as he hovered over me, waiting.

"Teach me, Easton," I finally whispered, tears slipping down my cheeks. "I want to soar." With a grin as wicked as the gleam in his desire-filled eyes, he easily lifted me into his arms and took me to his bedroom, where he showed me all night long just how much he loved my body.

* * *

BLINDING white light pressed against my eyelids, making me force them open. He'd forgotten to close the blinds again.

"East," I groaned, patting his side of the bed only to find it cold and empty. Sitting up, I noticed he had dressed me in one of his big shirts. "East?" I called again, and he stuck his head out of the bathroom, shaving cream on his face. He grinned.

"Ready for more already?" He winked and ducked when I threw a pillow at him. "How about after breakfast?"

"Why aren't you in bed with me? We should be sleeping and having sex all day," I moaned, watching desire pool in his gaze for me.

"Tempting, but I have work."

"Speaking of, you still haven't told me about it." I got out of bed and raised my arms above my head, stretching the stiffness out of my neck and back. His shirt lifted up, exposing my bare butt, causing him to groan.

"I'm sure they won't mind if I'm a few minutes late. Come shower with me, Harley. Let me make you sing one more time."

Because I couldn't resist this man, I took his invitation and sang his name like it was my greatest prayer.

At his kitchen counter thirty minutes later, he was guzzling down a cup of coffee while I picked at a bowl of cereal under his watchful gaze.

"Have you thought about therapy?" He wasn't looking at me as he voiced the question I'd been dreading.

"I tried it a few times," I whispered, dropping my spoon in the half-full bowl and pushed it away.

"Did anyone ever go with you?" He was gripping the counter now, his intense gaze on me.

"What do you mean?" I stood, taking my bowl to the sink and tossing the soggy cornflakes.

"Has anyone ever supported you, Harley? Your mom? Dad? Friends?" I opened my mouth to tell him to shove his question up his ass, but then I saw the concern in his features.

I sighed. "No. They ridiculed me. Mom yelled; the therapist yelled. Everyone just didn't understand." He nodded, taking the bowl from me and putting it in the dishwasher.

"Will you go with me? Will you try again with me?" Sniffling, I scrunched up my nose and blinked away the tears threatening to fall.

"East, you don't have to do this. Really." I hugged myself, trying and failing to be in control of my emotions.

He stepped into me, backing me against the counter. A tear slid down my cheek, and he kissed it away. "Except I do. I'm not letting you suffer alone. You aren't alone anymore." He brushed his lips with mine. "You have me."

Chapter Twenty

EASTON

"YOU REALLY DON'T HAVE TO DO THIS," HARLEY whispered, fidgeting in her seat in the waiting room of the therapist I found for her. It wasn't easy to get this appointment, but my parents built the home of the therapist, and it helped me skip the line. I still had to tell Harley about them; it was quickly becoming another secret between us. And we didn't do secrets.

I wasn't sure how she would react, given how her parents had treated her. I didn't want her to think that I had something she didn't, when, in reality, I'd grown up without these people. I hadn't needed them then, and I sure as hell didn't need them now.

Dropping my hand on her bouncing, jean-clad knee, I squeezed her small leg. "I'm not doing anything you wouldn't do for me," I reminded her, and she sighed in irritation.

"Really, East? This isn't funny. I am freaking out." She rested her head on my shoulder. I longed for her to suck my strength straight from my body. She needed every ounce for what she was about to do.

"It's going to be okay. I promise, it's all going to be okay."

"And if she can't fix me? If I'm so beyond repair? What then, Easton?" she whispered, panicked.

"You don't need to be fixed, Harley. That's not why we are here. I told you I'm not here to fix you. I'm here to heal you, little bird. You are not broken. Do you hear me?" I grasped her chin between my fingers, tilting her head toward mine.

Brushing my lips to hers quickly, her bouncing knee slowed, and then her name was called.

"Harley Cole?" a middle-aged woman in a pair of navy blue slacks and a white, ruffly, button-up top called her to the back. Harley stood, and nervously, her eyes darted between me and the lady.

"Can he come with?" she tentatively asked, reaching for me.

"It's up to you, Miss Cole." Squeezing Harley's hand, I gained her attention and shook my head.

"You need to do this without me. I'll be right here waiting for you. If you really need me, I'll be in there in a heartbeat. You are strong enough to do this on your own, to heal yourself." She nodded and blinked away her tears.

"To heal myself," she repeated with a firm nod, and then like the beautiful bird she was, she raised her head high and followed the lady, her hair gleaming in the fluorescent light like the most exquisite feathers.

I scrolled through the new phone Andy and Layla gave me. Harley signed me up for all the latest social media apps, but nothing piqued my interest. I didn't want to follow anyone from my past; nobody was worthwhile. The device vibrated with a text message, surprising me.

Andy: *How is she?*

I'd filled him in on Harley and the need for a therapist better suited to her condition. He and Layla had been instrumental in finding the therapist, and for that, I was grateful. But I still struggled to let them in, to give them the closure they needed.

Easton: *Nervous.*

They'd asked me yesterday if I wanted to change my name and take theirs. I'd left the office immediately, unsure of how to respond. I'd only known them for a couple of weeks, and they were already asking me to change it.

Harley would know what to do. She was my voice of reason.

Andy: *Why don't you bring her by for dinner at the house tonight?*

I'd been invited a few times for dinner, and somehow had found a good reason not to go every time. I could easily say no, tell him she couldn't handle it, but she'd tell me to go. Just like I pushed her here.

Easton: *I'll ask her.*

Andy: *Let me know. Your mother would love to cook for the two of you.*

They constantly referred to themselves as mother and father, but they didn't have a clue on how to be either. A real mother never would have deserted me.

Harley stepped back into the waiting room an hour later, her cheeks flushed, eyes swollen, her bottom lip bruised from biting it. Standing, I opened my arms, and she walked into them, dropping her head to my chest with a soft cry.

"I did it," she whispered, relieved.

"I knew you could. How does it feel to fly, little bird?" I sank my fingers into her thick hair, pressing a kiss to her forehead. She sighed in my hold.

"Freeing."

"Just wait until you soar."

* * *

IT WAS my turn to squirm in my seat in the car. Harley's hand was interlocked with mine on the center console. She was humming along to the song playing on the radio, her other hand dancing in the wind of the open windows.

She hadn't been this happy in a long time.

"Something's bothering you. What's wrong?" She turned her head to me, giving me all of her attention.

"Why would something be wrong?" I decided telling her was a bad idea, not after the day she'd had.

"You're tense. What's going on? Is it today? Are you regretting coming?" Worry and panic didn't belong in her tone, but it was there, and I hated that I was the reason it was.

"I don't regret anything that I do with or for you, Harley. Don't you ever forget that. It's about my birth parents." I sighed, pressing the button to bring up the windows on the car so we didn't have to talk so loudly.

"Oh? I didn't realize you'd found them."

"They found me. They own Andy's Construction and have been looking for me for years, apparently. They gave me the job, apartment, car, phone, all of it in some fucked up way of mending their mistakes." I glanced at her. She was digesting the new information.

"So, you've known for a couple of weeks then. Were you afraid to tell me?" I pulled into the parking garage of our apartment. She unclipped her seatbelt and turned to me.

Squeezing the steering wheel, I shifted the car into park and glared at the concrete wall in front of us.

"I didn't want to upset you with how your parents have been." She nodded.

"Why are you telling me now, then?"

"They want us to come for dinner." I groaned, letting go of her hand to run it through my hair. I needed a haircut.

"Let's go. It won't hurt to get to know them." She reached for me, taking my hand in both of hers. "Hiding from the truth will only hurt you in the long run, East. I'd kill for my parents to invite us over for dinner. Plus, if it backfires in our face, we have each other, right?" The grin that tugged at my lips belongs to Harley Cole.

"You bet. You and me against the world, little bird."

Pulling out my phone, I shot a text off to Andy.

Easton: *We'll be there. What time?*

His response was instant, and I rolled my eyes at his desperation.

Andy: *Now?*

I showed Harley the text message. Throwing her head back with laughter, her eyes glowed with happiness. "Why the hell not? I'm starving."

"I love you." Leaning across the console, I cupped her face, pulling her closer to me. I softly bit down on her bottom lip, drawing out a loud moan from deep in her throat. Licking the sensitive flesh, her fingers dug into my scalp, pulling at my hair.

"More. So much more," she whispered against my lips just as I began to devour her mouth, stealing and claiming her breath as my own.

* * *

I FOLLOWED the directions to the large house on the other side of town. Harley looked on in amazement and then threw the comment I'd been waiting for. "You never mentioned they were stinking rich. I'm totally underdressed." She glanced down at her ripped jeans and casual t-shirt.

"I disagree. I was thinking you're wearing too much and should take off your shirt." She slapped my chest while laughing.

"You're insatiable. We are not doing anything of the sort in your parents' driveway. Now, be the man I fell in love with, not the guy who was betrayed by everyone. I showed you that you can trust. You trust me, right?" I nodded, bringing her hand to my lips and kissing the soft skin.

"With my life."

"Then trust me to protect you tonight. Nobody's getting through me." Taking the deepest breath I could muster, I exited the car and rounded the front. Opening the door for Harley she took my hand and squeezed.

She led me to the front door like it wasn't her first time here and rang the doorbell. Glancing up at me, she smiled, and from the furrow in her perfect brows, I knew she was waiting for me to do the same.

Layla threw open the door in a floor-length blue dress the same color as our eyes. She smiled at Harley and leaned forward to give her a hug.

"It's so nice to meet you, honey," she said, and Harley teared up at the embrace.

"Oh, you, too." There was a slight wobble in her voice, but then she cleared her throat. But I saw the longing in her eyes.

"East, honey. I've missed you." Layla embraced me as well, and Harley let go of my hand, giving me space to hug my mother.

One stern look from Harley, and I was wrapping my arms around Layla, hugging her back. She gasped before squeezing me as tight as she possibly could.

"You have such a beautiful home," Harley said, making Layla pull away. She wiped at her eyes and then turned her attention to Harley.

"Andy built it for us a few years ago. We make a good team. He's the architect, and I'm the interior designer." She laughed, smoothing her hands down her dress. I watched her and Harley interact, listening to their easy conversation, and fell in love with Harley all over again.

Andy greeted us in the kitchen. He slapped me on the shoulder before pulling Harley into a big squeeze. This time, she did cry and apologized quickly, her cheeks flaming in embarrassment.

"If you'll excuse me, I just need the restroom." Layla offered to show her where it was, and I was stuck with Andy, wondering if coming here today was the right idea for Harley.

"She's beautiful, son," Andy commented, calling me that fucking word again. The one he had no right to say.

"She's everything to me," I agreed, and he chuckled.

"Felt the same way about your mother. It's crazy how you just know when they're the one. Are you going to propose?" He asked, grabbing me a water from the fridge. He must have sensed my hesitation to answer, because he took a long swig from his before saying, "I know it's none of my business. I know I wasn't there when you needed me, but Easton, I'm here now. I'm doing the best I can, and I understand why you're pushing me away. I just need you to know I'm here if you need someone."

"Why didn't you have anymore kids?" The question that had been nagging at my head for the last few weeks finally voiced itself. I had to know.

"When I turned twenty-one, I had been working for a small construction company and had enough saved to buy a small home for me and Layla. She had been working double, sometimes triple shifts between the furniture store and diner she worked at." He pauses to finish his beer.

"Our goal was to save enough money to give you a better life than we had. We went back to the adoption agency to find you. But you were in a foster home, and they wanted to evaluate us to see if we were able to provide a good, stable environment. We passed almost all the tests, but then your mother was fired from the diner after your grandfather came and trashed the place looking for Layla. Without that income, we couldn't afford the mortgage payments and the wellbeing of a child."

"So, you left me," I finished for him, rage boiling inside me. *Where the hell was Harley?*

"We left you in the care of a good foster family. They let us come see you whenever we wanted. I'm surprised you don't remember us."

"I was four. What the hell did you want me to remember?"

"Your mother used to sing you this song about pigs. Do you remember that?" he pushed, and I tried to think back to that foster family. They were kind people until the father died in a car accident, and we were all sent to other foster families.

"The mother used to sing a song to put me to sleep. She used to play with my toes."

"That was me," Layla said from the hallway, a tear rolling

down her cheek. Harley was at her side, watching the scene unfold. "This little piggie went to the market..."

Her voice triggered a memory, and I staggered back. "East?" Harley was at my side, her hands latched onto my forearm, grounding me.

"It was you, but then why didn't you come back?!" I shouted, slamming my fist down on the marble counter.

"We did, but by then, the adoption agency had been burned down, and you had been adopted," Andy finished the story, but I shook my head.

"You never answered my first question. Why didn't you have any more?"

"I didn't want another child if I couldn't have you." Layla wiped at the tears rolling down her cheeks, and I hated the anger flowing through my veins.

"I need some air." Leaving the suffocating kitchen, I stepped outside to the pool area and sucked in a much-needed breath of fresh air.

"What would you do?" I asked Harley, already knowing her fucking answer but needing to hear it, nonetheless.

"Forgive them," she whispered, her fingers lacing with mine, her lips at my shoulder, her strength wrapping around me.

"They left me." The words were broken as they left my lips.

"They came back. Mine haven't come back, East." I nodded, mulling over her words. "They love you and only want the best for you."

"What did she say to you?" I squeezed her hand, acknowledging her words.

"Nothing. She hugged me and consoled me the way I wish my mother would."

"I'd like to think, if they had come back into my life, you wouldn't be here today. Everything happens for a reason, right? We wouldn't have met." Harley laughed.

"You are crazy, certifiably crazy." I pulled her into my chest, burying my head in her shoulder, hiding my face in her hair.

"As long as you love me, I don't care."

"We were meant to find each other, East, just like they were meant to find you. Forgive them, love them, let them in." She kissed my ear, her lips soft and gentle.

"Okay," I agreed, and she pulled back, looking at me with bright, excited eyes.

"How does it feel to fly, East?" She bit her lip to hide her grin, and I threw my head back and laughed.

"Like I'm finally alive, little bird."

Epilogue

HARLEY

DAYS TRICKLED INTO WEEKS, AND THEN WEEKS trickled into months. The summer humidity evaporated as hurricane season threatened to ruin our tropical paradise, and then that too was gone with harsh winds that made any true Floridan's knees shake from the early morning freezing temperatures. Luckily for us, the sunshine state was never cold for long, with temperatures picking up in the afternoon.

Easton had surprised me the day after Thanksgiving with the biggest artificial Christmas tree I had ever laid my eyes on. He put it up right in the center of our apartment, and let me choose all the decorations. Together, we spent hours picking out ornaments for the tree, and then decorating it took an entire weekend, but every time I looked at it, at all the glittering lights and sparkling ornaments, my heart swelled with love.

I had grown up with what I termed a colorful Christmas. My parents didn't care for a theme, and thinking back on it now, it must have looked horrendous to all the friends I brought home during those few weeks.

Sitting on the couch now, surrounded by the white winter land Easton had created for me, I sipped slowly on the piping hot chocolate in my cold hands, the fake fireplace crackling in the background. White and gold-wrapped presents were tucked perfectly under the tree, and now, I was waiting for East to come home from work.

The job he had been gifted had turned out to become his biggest passion. He loved to build and had proven his worth to everyone in the company by becoming a lead foreman. Andy and Layla wanted to give him the world, but he wanted to work for what he had, so he started at the bottom of the ladder on the cleaning crew for job sites and slowly worked his way up.

He even took over the monthly payments for the apartment and gave them back the car they gifted, choosing to buy an old F-150 that he spent Saturday mornings cleaning and working on.

Bing Crosby's voice crooned about a White Christmas from the speaker I set up in the kitchen, sending a chill across my skin, goosebumps rising in their wake. Bundling up in a fluffy white blanket, I closed my eyes, trying to take it all in.

The fresh scent of chocolate chip cookies wafted in the air from the batch I just put in the oven, and I sighed. I made it. I found my one great love. I survived school and college, and with baby steps, I was overcoming my bulimia. The only thing missing was my crazy boyfriend.

My phone rang from the kitchen counter, and I ignored it, too comfortable to move. It was probably Kennedy calling to tell me about her new boyfriend, some hotshot millionaire lawyer she'd found in Miami. Surprisingly, we stayed in contact, and despite our rocky start, she'd turned out to be a good friend.

Easton's keys jiggled in the lock. Looking over the back of the couch, I watched him enter, balancing a box of pizza and a few gift bags. He toed off his work boots and then winked at me, his face flushed from the cold front that had rolled in this morning, just in time for Christmas.

"Smells good in here, bird." He walked over to me, dropping a kiss to my head before putting his things down on the kitchen counter.

"I made your favorite," I told him, and he grinned, his eyes lighting up with glee.

"Give me five minutes. We got soaked out there today." He headed into our bedroom, and the shower started a second later. While he was in the shower, the timer blared through the large space, and I quickly got up to take out the cookies from the oven, their heavenly scent overwhelming.

"You really shouldn't have." He was suddenly at my back, arms caging me in against the cold counter, his lips kissing a trail of fire across my skin.

"That was quick." I giggled, sinking back into his warm body.

"Didn't want to waste any time with you." He turned me in his arms, and I immediately wrapped my arms around his neck. Standing on my toes in my red fuzzy socks, I pressed a soft kiss to his damp lips. "You taste like hot chocolate, baby. So, fucking delicious," he groaned against my lips, his fingers digging into my hips.

"I missed you today," I whispered, brushing my nose against his, inhaling his clean scent. The stubble from his day-old beard burned my skin in the most erotic way, his lips teasing against mine, a promise of what was to come.

"I miss you every day, bird." He always knew what to say to make my heart soar.

"Our first Christmas together couldn't be more perfect." Closing my eyes, I leaned into him, his warmth surrounding me. He hummed in agreement and pecked my lips again before pulling away.

"The pizza's getting cold, baby. Plus, I want to eat those cookies." His hungry gaze focused behind me on the sheet of chocolate chip cookies. "I can't believe you made my favorite." He pulled the pizza blade out of the drawer and sliced the boring old cheese pizza into big slices. I handed him a plate, and together, we devoured the large pizza, not even making it to the dining table.

"I applied for another job today," I informed him after putting my empty plate in the dishwasher. I hadn't had any luck finding a job. All the local newspapers weren't hiring or were going digital, so I started applying for other editorial jobs.

"You know you don't have to work right? I make enough to support us both." He reminded me of this fact every time I brought up my worry of being jobless.

"I need to find something to do. I'm going crazy just sitting here," I reminded him, and he nodded in understanding.

"I can see if there are any openings at the office next week," he suggested, but I shook my head, following him to the couch, a plate of still-warm cookies in my hands. He flopped on the couch and turned the flat screen on, looking up at me with a hunger that surpassed the freshly-baked cookies.

"Your parents have done enough for us. I couldn't think of asking for more. I need to do this on my own. Otherwise, my degree will have been all for nothing." He opened his arms, and I settled in beside him. He then tucked the blanket around us.

"That degree wasn't for nothing. It brought us together. Don't you ever forget that, bird." He picked up two cookies from the plate and ate them both in a few bites. He moaned his delight, instantly turning me on. "Best fucking cookies ever."

"You say that every time," I laughed, taking a bite from my own.

"You make them better every time, I swear." He found us a classic Christmas movie to watch, and then we snuggled closer together, not knowing where one started and the other ended.

His steady heartbeat lulled me to sleep halfway through the movie I had seen at least a hundred times, and he held me tighter. "I love you so much, my little bird."

I was about to tell him how infinite my love was for him, but between the security of being wrapped in his arms, his scent invading all my senses, and his declaration of love, I sank into a deep, content sleep.

Easton

Harley softly snored against my chest, her lips parted ever so slightly, deep breaths blowing against my skin. I watched the gentle rise and fall of her chest. This tiny woman had crashed through my defenses one by one until she left me unarmed and ready for the kill.

She showed me love in a world I was so sure could never be kind. She gave me peace among the chaos, but most importantly, she taught me how to trust with unyielding faith.

The credits of whatever Christmas movie I'd picked blanketed us in darkness, and I took the moment to steal a kiss. She didn't wake as my lips brushed hers. Instead, a moan escaped her throat.

"Always singing for me, little bird." Moving her ever so carefully, I slipped away from the couch to our bedroom, where I got ready with her first Christmas gift.

The digital clock in the room shined brightly in the darkness. With two minutes until midnight, I quickly changed into the red velvet suit, adjusted the matching hat, and slid the gold glasses onto the bridge of my nose.

She once told me she loved ole Saint Nick. Hopefully, she would love me just as much. Pocketing the black velvet box into my pants pocket, I held up her letter, the one where she told me how much she hated the holidays without her parents.

I'd give her new memories. I would make her love Christmas again.

Tucking her letter back into my drawer, I exited the room. Tiptoeing through the apartment, I put a few surprise gifts under the tree for her, stole another one of her delicious cookies, then kneeled on the floor in front of the couch.

"Wake up, bird," I whispered, gently stroking her arm. She groaned, hiding her face in the blanket. "Ho, ho, ho." I rolled my eyes at my stupidity, but she pulled the blanket away from her face and slowly blinked, her beautiful eyes going wide with surprise.

"Santa?" she whispered, her lips curving into my favorite smile.

"I hear you've been a very good girl, Harley. Is that true?" She sat up, stretching her arms over her head. The blanket dropped, showing her exposed stomach where her shirt rode up. I licked my lips at the sight of her creamy skin.

She held my heated gaze with a mix of desire and determination. I was so fucking hooked on this woman. She could laugh, and I'd be hard for her.

"Oh, I'm not sure, Mr. Claus. You'd have to ask my boyfriend that one, and he seems to have disappeared." The rasp in her voice nearly unraveled me.

The ball was entirely in her court as she stole it, capturing me with the way she bit her bottom lip, waiting for my answer.

"Such a shame to leave you on the most magical night of the year," I whispered, and she nodded, her eyes dilating with lust.

"So terrible of him. I hope you give him coal." I laughed on a rushed exhale, and she grinned.

"And what do you want, my sweet little bird?" she pretended to ponder, tapping her chin and staring at the ceiling before looking back at me.

"You." Giving me little time to react, she launched herself at me, and I fell to my back, her perfect thighs straddling me.

"That's it, little bird. Take what you want." I barely recognized my own voice, so thick with desire as she palmed my hard cock through the velvet pants. I kneaded her ass, stroking my cock against her.

I was so ready for her, I could have slid right in, but I needed this to last longer. I had so much more planned for her tonight than a quick fuck.

"You're so fucking beautiful, Harley. You know that? I want to hear you sing for me, baby." She moaned, her hands reaching for my waistband and tugging the pants down.

"Easton," she whined. Her blue and green eyes had a fire in them as she writhed against me. "Please, I need you."

I growled and yanked down my pants and underwear in one

swift movement. Pulling my cock out, I wasn't willing to deny her. "You have me, little bird. I'm all yours."

She stood, pushing her sweatpants off, leaving her standing in front of me in a tight, white, knit long-sleeve shirt and a bright fucking red thong.

"Off. Take it all fucking off." I leaned up on my elbows, watching her undress for me. Her movements were jerky and rushed as she tore the shirt off her head, a white bra, holding her creamy breasts from my view.

She made quick work of the lace, throwing it behind her in her haste, and then her fingers wrapped around her thong. Her heated gaze locked on mine as she slowly tugged them over her ripe ass and down her toned thighs until the red lace dropped to the floor.

"Come take what you need, Harley," I rasped, and she moaned. Dropping to her knees, she lifted herself up before sliding down on my hard cock, both of us moaning in sync. She twisted and rolled against me, and I pinched her clit while holding and kneading her breasts.

"East!" she moaned my name, and I nearly came just from the need in her voice.

"Maybe I should let you ride me more often, give you all the fucking control. Is that what you like?"

"Oh, fuck." She wasn't capable of answering the question as an orgasm tore through her. My name fell from her lips like the most beautiful song I'd ever heard.

Her hips moved up and down on me as she worked herself through her orgasm. I watched in awe, trying to stay rigid as possible rather than moving with her. I wasn't ready for this to end. I planned to fuck her all night long.

Her erratic breathing increased even more when I pinched her clit one more time, and a second orgasm rippled through her. Her hips bucked faster when I moved one thumb back and forth over her sensitive clit. "That's it, my little bird. Keep singing for me." Sitting up, I latched onto her neck, leaving open-mouth kisses along the exposed skin, her pulse jumping beneath my touch.

"Easton, please!" she screamed, a frustrated growl following my name. I watched pleasure overtake the fire of desire in her eyes, only to be relit when I sucked on her neck.

"You are so fucking beautiful with your wet pussy weeping all over my cock, Harley." I held her head up as her neck rolled, her eyes struggling to stay focused.

"Please, Easton, let go. Fly with me." Her rasped words, hooded eyes, and almost limp body were my undoing.

"Fuck, Harley," I groaned, thrusting deep into her over and over again, making her mine like it was the first time. I lost myself in her, pumping my hot cum into her tight body. "Fuck. Fuck. Fuck," I groaned into her sweaty neck.

We collapsed to the floor, her body draped over mine, both of us struggling to catch our breath.

"Santa Claus, huh?" She giggled, body shaking with laughter.

"I wanted to give you a new memory," I whispered, stroking her silky hair.

"I wasn't expecting that at all."

"Merry Christmas, little bird." I pressed a soft kiss to her temple. "But I need you to sit up for the second half of your first Christmas memory with me." She instantly sat up, her eyes narrowing.

"Okay. What do you have up your sleeve?"

"Not coal." She threw her head back, her laughter surrounding us.

Picking up my discarded pants, I felt for the little box, and finally, my fingers wrapped around it. Taking a deep breath, I showed it to her. Opening the small lid, the diamond ring I'd picked out for her glittered in the light from the twinkling Christmas tree.

"Not coal," she softly agreed, her eyes darting between me and the ring. She noticeably swallowed, almost as though she was the nervous one.

"I thought I would ask you on your favorite day of the year. Will you marry me and become Mrs. Briggs, my sweet little bird?" Her eyes widened more, if possible, at the mention of my real last name.

I hadn't told her that I had gone and changed it.

"East, are you sure?" she whispered, her trembling hands circling my neck.

"I wouldn't have asked if I wasn't."

"Of course, I'll marry you. There's nothing I want more than to be your wife. To be your little bird for eternity."

Sliding the ring on her finger, she stared at it in wonder.

"It's real. I'm going to be yours forever," she whispered.

Cradling her face in my hands, I wiped away her tears, kissing her cheeks, nose, and the bow of her top lip. "You've always been mine. I was never going to let you go, little bird."

Pressing my lips to hers, I inhaled her soft cries, and I kissed her breathless.

"Now, time to hear you sing again, my little bird. You know how much I love your song."

THE END

I HOPE YOU ENJOYED Little Bird! Want a peek into Easton's and Harley's future? Subscribe to my mailing list and you'll get instant access to an exclusive bonus scene!

Bonus Scene

Ten Years Later

"Tell me again, Mommy! Tell me again!" Quinn's ice-blue eyes widened as she looked up at me, her black hair pulled back into a messy ponytail.

"It's bedtime, sweetheart." I softly untangled the hair tie from her wild hair and tucked her back into bed.

"I'll never be able to sleep without knowing the ending." She yawned, rubbing her eyes with two small fists.

"How about if Daddy tells you." Looking over my shoulder, Easton stood there, eyes red, body sagging with exhaustion, yet a bright smile tugged at his lips for his little angel.

"Daddy! You're home!" she squealed, jumping right out of bed and throwing herself into her daddy's strong arms.

He caught her like he always did and spun her around the room, her loud giggles bouncing off the pink walls.

A moment later, he was tucking her back into bed and sitting beside me, his hand reaching for mine, calloused fingers wrapping around mine.

"Which story is Mommy telling you tonight?" Quinn looked between us with her daddy's eyes and scrunched her tiny nose.

"The one about the pen pals." She crossed her arms, glaring at me for not finishing our love story.

"Well, what did she tell you?" Easton glanced at me, and then winked at our six-year-old daughter, who thought she had more wisdom than East and I combined.

"How they wrote love letters, and then one day, they met and fell in love like it ain't nobody's business," she prattled off, recounting insignificant details of the story to her father.

"So, what more do you need to know?" she sighed in exasperation.

"Did they get married? Live in a castle? How about kids? Did they have those? And what about living happily ever after? I have so many questions!" she exclaimed.

"What do you know about all those things?" he suspiciously asked, and she rolled her big, blue eyes and huffed.

"Dad, are you kidding? Do you know anything? I watch TV. Duh." I couldn't hold in my laughter at the sass. She was a perfect combination of me and Easton. Together, we made a beautiful little girl.

And once we got her to bed, I would surprise him with the news of another baby, the one growing in my stomach right now. Placing my hand on my still flat belly, I watched as East answered all her silly questions and then kissed her goodnight once she eventually tuckered out.

"She loves you so much," I whispered, watching her sleep through the crack of the door from the hallway.

"She's the best gift you could have ever given me, little bird." He pressed a kiss to my head, pulling me into his embrace. I sank into his hard chest.

"The best, huh?" I looked up, kissing his stubbled jaw. His father had been grooming him to take over the construction company so he and Layla could travel the world. Easton had been working long hours to learn everything. We hadn't had very much alone time recently.

"Besides giving me yourself? Yeah, she's the best, Harley. I never thought I would have space in my heart for more than you, but then you gave me her, and my heart grew."

"It better grow some more." I smiled into his neck, softly kissing his hammering pulse. He pulled back, looking at me with wide eyes and then at my stomach.

"You're pregnant?" he exclaimed, and I quickly pressed my finger to his lips, shushing him.

"Don't wake her. Otherwise, we can't celebrate." I winked, and he picked me up, my legs immediately wrapping around his waist. My arms wound around his neck, hands sinking into his thick, dark hair.

"You're the gift that just keeps on giving, little bird," he murmured, and I melted into him. God, how I loved this man— more than my next breath.

"I love you, Easton."

"I love you, little bird."

Thank You!

Thank you for reading *Little Bird,* a pen pal, age-gap romance. I hope you enjoyed your adventure with Easton and Harley! Please consider leaving a review on Amazon/Goodreads! They really help authors like me SO MUCH!!!

Also by Taylor Jade

Stand-alone:

My Military Hero

My Beast

Summer at the Ranch

Merry Christmas, Soldier

The Stowaway

Hired Heartbreaker

Rescuer

Can I Be Him

The Vine Claus

Loving You Series:

Nobody But You

Only You

Summer With You

Christmas With You

Forbidden Series:

Our Forbidden Love

Dexter Brothers:

Always My Hero

Always My Protector

Always My Savior

Always My Comfort

Made in the USA
Monee, IL
29 May 2025

18437509R00080